A Wild Goose Chase
Christmas

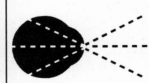

This Large Print Book carries the
Seal of Approval of N.A.V.H.

A WILD GOOSE CHASE CHRISTMAS

JENNIFER ALLEE

THORNDIKE PRESS

A part of Gale, Cengage Learning

GALE
CENGAGE Learning·

Detroit • New York • San Francisco • New Haven, Conn • Waterville, Maine • London

GALE
CENGAGE Learning®

Copyright © 2012 by Jennifer AlLee.
Thorndike Press, a part of Gale, Cengage Learning.

ALL RIGHTS RESERVED
The persons and events portrayed in this work of fiction are the creations of the author, and any resemblance to persons living or dead is purely coincidental.
Thorndike Press® Large Print Clean Reads.
The text of this Large Print edition is unabridged.
Other aspects of the book may vary from the original edition.
Set in 16 pt. Plantin.

LIBRARY OF CONGRESS CATALOGING-IN-PUBLICATION DATA

AlLee, Jennifer.
    A wild goose chase Christmas / by Jennifer Allee.
        pages ; cm. — (Thorndike Press large print clean reads) (Quilts of love series)
        ISBN 978-1-4104-5610-6 (hardcover) — ISBN 1-4104-5610-2 (hardcover)
    1. Quiltmakers—Fiction. 2. Older men—Fiction. 3. Heirlooms—Fiction. 4. Christmas stories. 5. Large type books. I. Title.
PS3601.I39W55 2012
813'.6—dc23   2012045450

Published in 2013 by arrangement with Abingdon Press

Printed in the United States of America
1 2 3 4 5 6 7 17 16 15 14 13

To my grandmother, Marie Staats,
who is dancing and laughing in heaven

ACKNOWLEDGMENTS

Each book presents its own unique challenges and blessings, and this one was no different. Big thanks are due to so many:

- To my family, who never questioned why I couldn't be separated from my laptop for two solid months. You guys rock!
- To my awesome agent, Sandra Bishop, for never letting me lose hope. Ever!
- To Lisa Richardson and Susie Dietze, for making themselves available for quick critiques and feedback as I worked my way through Izzy's story.
- To Abingdon acquisitions editor Ramona Richards, for her encouraging words and support.
- To Teri, for her loving care in editing the final manuscript.
- To the Abingdon sales and marketing teams, for everything they've done to

make the Quilts of Love series a success.

- And, of course, thanks to God in heaven, the giver of all good things. He's given me more good things than one gal deserves. I am blessed.

1

Izzy Fontaine was up to her elbows in family photos when the doorbell rang. The sound echoed, joined by two sharp barks and the clicking of nails on the hardwood floor as Bogie rounded the corner, bounded across the room, and slid to a stop in front of the door. The Jack Russell terrier did the same thing anytime someone rang the bell. And every time the door opened and he saw it wasn't his owner, he slunk out of the room with his head down.

Izzy looked down at the dog. "I miss her, too, Boy."

Letting out a sigh, she dropped the eight-by-tens from her hands, pushed her chair away from the table, and trudged across the room. Who would stop by unannounced? A list of the usual suspects flitted through her mind: Students selling magazine subscriptions? Local proselytizers unnecessarily worried about her soul? Or the man with the pickup truck full of gardening tools who kept offering to rake the leaves from her yard? What she didn't expect to see through the fisheye lens of the peephole was a senior citizen standing on the porch.

She opened the door wide enough to stick her head through but blocked the bottom of the opening with her body to keep Bogie from running outside. "Can I help you?"

The man smiled. "Are you Isabella Fontaine?"

The rational part of her brain, the part that took copious mental notes whenever she watched TV crime dramas, warned her against divulging personal information to a stranger. But the other part, the part that usually found the best in everyone, couldn't believe this sweet old man held any danger.

"Yes, I'm Isabella. But no one calls me that."

"What do they call you?"

"Izzy."

The sides of his wiry white mustache rose in a smile. "Well then, Izzy it is. I'm Virgil, and I believe I'm the one who can help you." With a bit of difficulty he produced a huge ribbon-tied box from behind his back and held it up in front of him.

"What is that?"

"A present for you. From your grandmother."

Izzy pulled back as if the box had grown teeth and snapped at her. Two days ago, alone at the assisted living facility, Grandma Isabella had passed from this world to the next. Guilt still gnawed at Izzy for not being there when her grandmother needed her. This unexpected gift only made things worse.

"Can I bring it in?"

Virgil's hopeful question reclaimed Izzy's attention. She hesitated, but the crack of thunder, followed several seconds later by a flash of lighting across the cloud-filled sky, made up her mind. "Oh. Of course." She stepped back and opened the door wider. "Come in."

With slow but steady steps, Virgil entered the house. His eyes took in the dark wood and built-in cabinetry so typical of a craftsman house. "It's just as beautiful as Isabella described it."

"Gran loved her house." Only it wasn't Gran's house anymore; it was Izzy's. Six months ago, when Gran fractured her hip and decided to move into the assisted living facility, Izzy convinced herself she was just taking care of Gran's house, Gran's dog. Just temporarily. But she couldn't keep telling herself that. Not anymore.

Virgil pointed to the heavy oak table in the dining area, strewn with photographs. "Are any of those of Isabella?"

"They all are." Izzy shut the door and followed Virgil, passing him and going to the table. "I'm making a photo display for Gran's funeral and I can't decide which picture to use. I narrowed it down to these." She grabbed two photos from the table and held them up for Virgil to see.

One was a black and white of a young Isabella in a classic dance pose. She balanced on one leg, satin-clad toes stretched into perfect pointe, her other knee drawn up, arms held out in front of her. The rapturous expression on her smooth, unblemished face and the extension of her fingertips gave the impression that she was reaching for her one true love.

The other picture was much different. It was a headshot, probably taken the last time her church updated the picture directory. She wore a burgundy sweater with a silk flower pinned to it, her silver hair pulled back into a tidy bun. This was an Isabella mellowed by time, her skin etched with lines, her smile content.

Two pictures representing two very different sides of the same woman. Izzy looked from one to the other and shook her head.

"I'm just not sure how she'd rather be remembered."

Virgil lowered himself into a hardback chair, leaning the box against one leg. "I think she'd like to be remembered both ways." He reached out and took the photo of young Isabella. "I know I could never forget her."

Just how well had Virgil known her grandmother? Izzy pulled out another chair and sat in front of him. "Were you and Gran . . . close?"

Virgil chuckled and waggled his finger at her. "Yes, but not in the way you're thinking. We had a lot in common. And believe me, when you live in a place like Vibrant Vistas, it's an accomplishment just finding someone who remembers enough about their past to compare notes."

Izzy laughed. "So if you two were such good friends, why didn't I ever see you when I was there?"

He swatted his hand in her direction. "You came there to see her, not to meet her doddering friends. I would have been in the way."

"Somehow, I doubt that." Izzy's eyes drifted back to the box at Virgil's side.

His eyes followed hers and he jumped in his chair. "Oh yes, the present. I'm sure

13

you're dying to get a look at it."

"I am curious."

He held it out to her. "Careful. It's heavier than it looks."

He wasn't kidding. She took it in both hands, glad for the warning. Laying it across her legs, she pressed her palms flat on the lid, as if doing so and concentrating would tell her what was inside. The last time she saw Gran, they'd decorated her room for Christmas, even though it was only the first of November. "If Walmart can put up their decorations months early," Gran had said, "then so can I. Besides, I'm not getting any younger. Christmas is my favorite holiday and I want to enjoy it as long as I can." She enjoyed it for a week, and then she was gone.

Had Gran known how little time she had left? If so, why hadn't she given Izzy the gift then, when they'd been together? Heat pushed against the back of Izzy's eyes as she looked down at the loosely tied, red satin ribbon, no doubt secured by Gran's arthritic fingers. Just one more experience Izzy had missed.

She looked up at Virgil, blinking quickly to keep the tears at bay. "Why did she give it to you?"

"She knew I'd keep it safe."

"Safe from what?"

"Not what. Who." Virgil's voice was low. He leaned forward, elbows to knees, eyes darting back and forth as if he expected to find covert operatives skulking in the shadows. "There are a lot of people who would like to get their hands on that."

She lifted her hands from the box. What in the world had Gran given her? "I don't understand. How could she have kept something valuable at the home without anybody finding out about it?"

"Not everybody recognizes true value when they see it." He nodded, impressed by the weight of his words.

"But what is it?"

He sat up straight, head slightly inclined. "It wouldn't be much of a present if I told you. Go on and open it."

Izzy grabbed one end of the satin ribbon, then froze. Maybe she should wait. It was a Christmas present, after all. Maybe she should save it until Christmas Day, just so she could share one last holiday with her grandmother.

But then that wouldn't honor Gran's spirit, would it? Gran never could wait to open gifts. She would have ripped into the package then and there.

The ribbon fell away with a yank, trailing

down her legs and brushing the floor. Wanting to make the moment last, she slowly lifted the white box top. Beneath it were neatly folded sheets of tissue paper. She peeled them away, one after the other, until her gift was revealed.

"Well," Virgil asked, "what do you think?"

"It's a quilt."

Izzy didn't mean for her voice to sound so flat and uninterested. But after the workup Virgil gave it, she expected something a little flashier.

"It's not just a quilt." A hint of scolding tinged his tone. "It's a family heirloom. That was one of Isabella's most prized possessions."

Izzy looked back down at the quilt. Triangles of different colors, mostly faded and worn by age, seemed to chase one another in geometric patterns, up one side and down the other. Izzy thought back to all the years she'd spent with her grandmother: long summer visits as a child, when she would pack her tiny pink suitcase and stay for a week at a time; so many weekends in her teen years, after her mother moved Izzy and her brother back to California and close to Gran; and those months after Izzy's accident, when Gran took her in and mended not only her body but her spirit as well. In

16

all that time, Gran never mentioned this quilt. Izzy had never seen it. How important could it really have been? For that matter, how had she managed to keep it hidden from her at Vibrant Vistas?

Izzy reached across the box and squeezed Virgil's hand. "It's lovely. Did she tell you anything about it?"

His face nearly glowed at the prospect of sharing his knowledge. "Oh yes. This is what you call a Wild Goose Chase pattern." He ran one finger carefully down the middle of a row of triangles. "According to Isabella —"

Virgil was cut short by the pealing of the doorbell. Bogie dashed around the corner, nearly crashing into Izzy's legs as she crossed the room. Then the bell rang again. The dog barked and turned in a circle. By the time the bell rang a third time, he'd added a little jump to the barking and circling.

"All right, already. I'm coming!" She dropped the quilt box on the coffee table, scooped Bogie up in one arm, and then lunged for the door before the button-happy person outside could strike again.

Maybe *happy* was the wrong word to use. The man standing outside, shoulders hunched against the gentle rain that had begun to fall, was anything but happy. Izzy decided to cut him off before he could launch into a sales pitch and become even more disgruntled when she didn't bite.

"Whatever you're selling, I'm not buying. Have a nice day."

His palm slapped against the door before she could shut it. "I'm not selling anything. I'm looking for my grandfather."

"Your grandfather? What makes you think . . . oh." Izzy looked over her shoulder. "Virgil, does this man belong to you?"

Virgil sighed as he pushed himself out of the chair. "How did you find me, Max?"

"I got a call from Vibrant Vistas. Something about you paying the shuttle driver to drop you off here."

"Who needs Big Brother when you've got Nurse Bauer and her minions?" Virgil mumbled as he ambled toward them.

The rain came down harder, and Max ducked his head as fat drops plopped on him from the roof's overhang. The soggier he got, the less imposing he seemed.

Izzy stepped back. "Come in out of the rain."

"Thanks." He swooped into the room, and a glimmer of a smile flashed at her, exposing a dimple in one cheek.

She closed the door and put Bogie down

on the floor. "Stay out of trouble," she said, scratching his ear. He scampered across the room and settled into a wingback chair facing the door, keeping watch in case any other unexpected visitors decided to show up. Izzy turned back to Max, ready to ask why he'd tracked down his grandfather, but the question died on her lips. He stood in the middle of her living room, staring down at the boxed quilt in shocked silence.

He pointed, his face reverting to its former unhappy self. "How did you get that?"

"Virgil brought it. It's a present from my grandmother."

Max shot her a look. "Isabella Randolph is your grandmother?"

"Yes." Izzy spoke slowly. "She gave me the quilt."

Max shook his head sharply, sending a fine spray of water in her direction. "Sorry, Miss, but she gave it to me first."

Virgil groaned. "Don't, Max."

Izzy's eyes swung from one man to the other. "Look, I don't know who you think you are, but —"

"I'm Max Logan, curator of the California Pioneer Museum. And that quilt," he said, stabbing his finger at the Wild Goose Chase, "is mine."

2

First, Virgil imagined a conspiracy surrounding the quilt, and now his grandson claimed it as his own. Obviously, delusion ran in their family. Izzy snatched the box up before Max could get any closer to it.

"The quilt is mine." She did her best to give him a down-her-nose, I-mean-business look, just like she'd seen her mother do a thousand times. "Since you're dripping all over my floor, I'd appreciate it if you'd leave."

As if they had rehearsed it, Virgil pulled a handkerchief from his pocket and held it out to Max, waving it near his face like a white flag. To her surprise, Max laughed. Not a lot, barely enough to shake his shoulders, really. But enough that she felt foolish over her reaction.

"Fine. I'll leave. For now." He ran the white cotton square across his face and over the back of his neck. "But I'll be back."

Izzy swallowed. "Why?"

"Because I have a letter of intent from Mrs. Randolph, proving she wanted me to have the quilt." His brows lowered, obscuring most of his chocolate-brown eyes. "I'll bring it by in the morning."

She pursed her lips, her defenses once again raised by his insistence. "I have school in the morning."

Surprise softened Max's features. "You're a student?"

"No, a teacher," she snapped. Why did everyone always think she was younger than she was? "I have to *teach* school in the morning."

"Oh, well, fine." He wadded up the handkerchief and stuffed it in the pocket of his slacks. "What time should I come over, then?"

"You can't. Not tomorrow. I'm busy after school."

He huffed out an exasperated breath. "Doing what?"

"Finalizing my grandmother's funeral." Max Logan was rude and insufferable, and only the fact that his grandfather stood beside him kept Izzy from saying so. "The funeral is on Saturday, and I doubt I'll want to talk to anyone on Sunday. So Monday is the best I can do."

The furrow in his brow deepened, and Izzy steeled herself for his argument. But Virgil intervened.

"Give it a rest, Max." He put his hand on the younger man's arm and gave it a squeeze. "The quilt's been meandering across the country for a hundred years. A few more days won't make any difference."

Max patted Virgil's hand, then removed it from his arm. "You're right. I can wait." He looked back at Izzy. "I'm sorry about your loss. Mrs. Randolph was quite a special lady."

Like a blade between her ribs, his comment brought up even more questions. Why had Gran never mentioned this man? How had the two of them become so close? And did she really promise to give him the quilt?

"Thank you." The words came out in a whisper.

Max nodded. "I'll be by Monday afternoon, then."

Izzy cleared her throat, wanting her next statement to be heard loud and clear. "I'd rather you not come here again."

"Excuse me?" Eyes narrowed, head cocked to the side and extended toward her, he resembled Bogie when he saw another dog on television.

"I'd rather meet you at your office." It occurred to Izzy that she didn't know anything about this man other than what he'd told her. She needed to make sure the museum he spoke about, and his position there, actually existed. "You do have an office, don't you?"

"Yes." Max bit the word off, letting her know what he thought of the implication behind her question. Beside him, Virgil snickered.

"Do you have a card?"

Without a word, he pulled his wallet from his back pocket, fished out a card, and handed it to her. She shifted the quilt box, holding it against her hip with one arm, took the card with her free hand, and ran her thumb over the embossed letters. *Max Logan, Director, California Pioneer Museum.* It certainly looked official.

"I'll see you Monday, then." She set the card on top of the quilt.

"Fine. Come on, Gramps." He motioned to Virgil with a jerk of his head, then stomped to the front door and yanked it open. The rain was coming down in sheets now. Without hesitating, Max took off his trench coat and held it out to his grandfather. "If you put this over your head, you should make it to the car without getting drenched."

23

So he did have a heart. In a moment, Izzy took in the broad shoulders beneath his sensible dress shirt, his tie knotted looser than it should be and listing to one side. He was a handsome man, no doubt about it. But what did her in was the expression on his face: the softening of his lips, the concern in his eyes as he took care of Virgil, even though Max obviously thought his grandfather had caused a lot of trouble today. And Izzy was sending them out into the rain. Who was heartless now?

"Wait."

Both men turned their heads toward her. She started to put the box down but thought better of it when she noticed Max leaning forward, hopeful that she'd changed her mind. She held up her hand, signaling for them to stay put, then jogged down the hall and rifled through the coat closet.

When she came back, she held the box clumsily against her chest with one arm and waived an umbrella in the air with her other hand. "Here you go."

"Gee, thanks." Max didn't seem impressed by her altruistic gesture.

His grandfather was another matter. "Thank you, Izzy." Before she knew it was coming, he grabbed her in a hug, squeezing tighter than she expected he could and crushing Gran's gift between them. Then he whispered in her ear. "Come visit me, and I'll tell you everything I know about the quilt."

Over his shoulder, she saw Max roll his eyes toward the ceiling. He'd heard, but she didn't want to let Virgil know that. The man was already certain he was being watched. No point in confirming it.

"I will," she whispered back. She handed him the umbrella. "Stay dry."

He grinned at her. "What's the fun in that?"

Max took his coat back and spread it over his head like a tarp. But when he made it to the threshold, he turned around one last time. "Take good care of it," he said, jutting his chin toward the quilt. "And don't do anything foolish, like putting it up on eBay."

Izzy had a few choice words for him but decided to keep them to herself. She stepped forward, putting her free hand on the side of the door. "Good-bye, Virgil. It was a pleasure meeting you."

They walked out and she shut the door behind them. A moment later, she heard whistling, then the opening lyrics of "Singing in the Rain." Izzy kneeled on the couch, setting the box beside her, and peeked out through the window sheers. Max strode quickly down the driveway, head down and steps sure, toward the curb where he'd parked his car. Virgil trailed behind doing a respectable Gene Kelly impression, swinging the open umbrella like a dance partner and purposely stomping into a puddle. With a chuckle, Izzy fell back against the cushions. What an odd pair those two were.

Her eyes rested on the quilt beside her. Speaking of odd pairs . . . why in the world had Gran decided to give her this quilt? If it was a family heirloom, shouldn't it go to Izzy's mother?

"Not if she wanted it to stay in the family," Izzy said to herself. If there was any monetary value in the quilt, her mother's first thought would be to sell it, and Gran would have known that. But could it really hold anything more than sentimental value? Carefully, Izzy lifted the heavy layers of material from the box. As she did, a folded piece of paper fell out and fluttered to the floor.

Izzy smiled. A message from Gran. Of course she wouldn't give Izzy a present with no card, no explanation at all. She picked up the paper, spread it out flat, and read.

My Sweet Izzy,
I've entrusted my dear friend Virgil with

26

this family heirloom. The fact that you are reading this means I've gone to Glory, and Virgil has given it to you. I'd hoped to do it myself, but obviously the Lord had other plans. You may be wondering why I chose to give you this gift. It is because I believe you are the one person who will truly appreciate it. The quilt holds the key to a treasure beyond price. It has a rich history, and by understanding it, you will have a richer, fuller future.

I pray the Lord will bless you and keep you until we are together again.

All my love,
Your Gran

Tears rolled unchecked down Izzy's cheeks. She gasped as the first one dropped from her chin and landed on the quilt, leaving a dark spot on the off-white background. If this was as old as she thought it was, it had no doubt seen its share of tears, but Izzy didn't want to add to them. She swiped the back of her wrist across her eyes and set the quilt to one side. Gran's letter hadn't told her much about the family heirloom, but it had reinforced two very important facts: first, her grandmother loved her. Second, there was no way on earth Max Logan was getting his hands on this quilt.

"If she thinks she can keep that quilt, she's crazy." Max shook his head and gripped the steering wheel a little tighter. He took a deep breath, trying to calm himself, but the smells of wet leather and Old Spice only made him more agitated. He glanced over at his grandfather. "Why'd you do it, Gramps?"

The older man fiddled with the heater vent. "Do what?"

"Why did you take her the quilt? You know full well Mrs. Randolph promised it to me."

"I know nothing of the sort. I know you and Isabella talked about it, how it was a historical piece as well as a family heirloom."

"Which is why she promised it to me."

"No. She didn't promise you anything."

"She gave me a letter."

"A letter, not a contract. She considered donating it to your museum. But in the end, she wanted her granddaughter to have it." Virgil shifted in his seat, angling himself toward Max. "If anyone should understand the importance of family and remembering those who came before us, it's you."

Max let out a sigh. "Of course I do. But that girl —"

"Woman. Izzy is a woman."

With her hair pulled back into a silky blond ponytail, her makeup-free face, and wide, innocent blue eyes, she had looked young, but Gramps was right. She was all woman. Still, it was hard to take her seriously. "What kind of a name is Izzy, anyway?"

"I think it's nice. Playful." Virgil's hands danced in front of him as if he conducted an orchestra. "I imagine more than one person called her grandmother by that name when she was young."

"I'm sure you're right. I stand corrected." Max agreed, but only to get off this rabbit trail and bring the conversation back to a more important topic. "What's eating at me is that Izzy doesn't even know what she has. It's an important piece of American history but she probably just sees it as an old bedspread."

"You don't know that." Virgil's hands dropped into his lap and he made a *tsk-tsk* sound. "You don't know anything about her."

They fell silent, but Max's brain never shut off. Gramps was right. He knew nothing about Izzy. He didn't even know her last name. If the study of history had taught him anything, it was the importance of getting to know your enemy. Not that he considered Izzy an enemy. But they were two people who both wanted the same thing and only one could come out the winner. It would be smart to learn as much about her as he could.

"So, Gramps," he said casually, "what did Mrs. Randolph tell you about Izzy?"

Max could hear the smile in his grandfather's voice when he answered.

"Everything."

3

Izzy was having a hard time concentrating on cubism, especially since her mind kept going back to triangles.

"This is Pablo Picasso, arguably one of the best-known cubist artists. But does he look anything like this man?" She clicked a button on the projector's wireless remote, changing the image on the screen at the front of the room. Several of the students laughed; a few made noises that loudly communicated their negative feelings toward the piece.

"No way that's the same guy," one of the boys said.

"It's supposed to be." Izzy walked up the aisle until she stood beside her desk and faced the class. "This is a portrait of Picasso done by Juan Gris, another popular cubist of the time. I want you to take a moment to study it."

Arms crossed, she looked at the picture

with her students, trying to imagine what a bunch of teenagers would think about such an unusual piece of art. But she kept zeroing in on the many triangles present in the painting. The background in particular was a series of triangles pointing in the same direction, giving it a feeling of movement.

Very much like her Wild Goose Chase quilt. The quilt that Max wanted. What was she going to do about Max? Did he really have a letter from Gran? And even if he did, was it binding? Would it give him any claim over the quilt?

The students started to whisper and fidget in their seats, signaling that the moment of silence had gone on long enough. She clapped her hands and looked back at the class. "What emotions do you feel when you look at this painting?"

"I feel nauseated." The remark came from the back of the room. Grant, her class clown and constant pot stirrer. If he wasn't so gifted, she wouldn't put up with his antics.

"Grant feels sick. Duly noted, although that isn't an emotion." Grant slouched in his seat as laughter rippled through the room. She pointed at a girl in the front row with her hand up. "Danielle?"

The girl stared at the portrait, tilting her head until her cheek nearly touched her shoulder. "It makes me feel sad."

"Why?"

"Because he looks like he had a stroke."

"I can see that," Izzy said, nodding. "The features on one side of the face are much weaker than on the other. Anyone else? Come on, just yell out the first thing that comes to your mind."

That did it. The room became a cacophony of short, shouted answers.

"Angry."

"Happy."

"Confused."

"Flying."

That one caught her attention. Flying. Like wild geese.

She moved to the switch panel on the wall, turning the lights on, off, and on again until order returned to the room. "Obviously, this style evokes many different emotions, as all good art should. Which is why each one of you is going to create a cubist-style self-portrait."

From the groans that came her way, Izzy guessed this wouldn't be her most popular assignment.

"Miss Fontaine?"

Josie's voice was so soft and timid that Izzy almost didn't hear her. She certainly hadn't seen the girl's hand barely raised above the height of her shoulder. But the fact that she spoke up at all was great progress. "Yes, Josie?"

"What medium should we use?"

"Any you want. Oils, charcoal, pastels, collage . . ."

"Macaroni," Grant threw out.

Izzy met his eyes and held them. "If you can find a way to manipulate macaroni into a cubist work of art, go for it." She stared at him a moment more in silence, then returned her attention to the class at large. "The idea is to stay true to the spirit of cubism."

"Over the weekend, I want you to do a preliminary sketch. As you know, you'll have a sub next week, but she'll help you work on your ideas. I'll be back after Thanksgiving and I expect you to knock my socks off." The bell rang, signaling the end of not only the class but of the school day as well. "Enjoy your holiday!" She had to yell to be heard over the commotion of teenagers scrambling to their feet, talking, gathering backpacks, and turning on cell phones.

In less than a minute, they were gone. Izzy smiled to herself as she made a sweep of the room, picking up trash and straightening chairs. Once upon a time, she'd been full of energy, just like those kids. Except that when she ran out of the classroom, her first thought hadn't been about what party to go to or where she'd hang out with her friends. It had been about the latest dance position she wanted to master or bit of choreography she struggled with. For years, she'd gone straight from one school to another, trading classrooms with desks and whiteboards for those with mirrored walls and ballet bars.

Izzy shook her head. Where had that come from? She rarely thought about those days. Getting ready for Gran's funeral must have stirred up the memories. Izzy had wanted so much to be like Gran, like the ballerina she'd seen in those old publicity pictures. And she almost was. She'd gotten so close.

With a sigh, she dumped into the garbage can the armful of litter she'd collected, then moved to the projector. Before she flipped the off switch, she took one last look at the Picasso portrait. Those prominent triangles really did remind her of flight. They transported her away from school and right back to her grandmother's quilt. Which brought her right back to the man she was trying not to think about.

"Max." Unthinking, she spoke his name on a puff of air.

"Who?"

Izzy spun around to see Barry Wilcox standing in the doorway. When had he come in? "Barry, you scared me."

"Sorry." He stepped toward her, cheeks slightly flushed. "Who's Max? If you don't mind me asking."

"What? Oh, no, of course not." Izzy knew full well that Barry had a crush on her. He was sweet, but after three years of teaching together she was no more romantically interested in him now than on the day they'd met. Playing up Max to be something he wasn't could be her key to moving out of Barry's sights. But it wouldn't be very nice to lie to him. "Max is assisting me with my grandmother's estate."

He frowned and tugged on the bottom of his sweater vest. "I was so sorry to hear about your grandmother, Izzy. Is there anything I can do?"

Izzy smiled, just enough to let him know she appreciated his concern but not so much as to encourage more attention.

"No, I'll be fine."

"OK." He nodded and turned for the door. Then he stopped and looked back. "Can I walk you to your car?"

"You go ahead. I have a few things to do here first."

Barry smiled and left. Izzy took her time

gathering her books and folders. Then she pushed the projector cart back into the audiovisual cabinet and locked it. A motorized rumble came from the parking lot. She looked out the window in time to see Barry's white VW Bug chugging by.

Snatching her bag off the desk, she gave the room one last look then rushed out the door and down the hall. If she hurried, she could get to the YMCA and fit in a good hour of water aerobics before it was time to meet her mother and brother at the church to go over the final details of Gran's funeral.

Izzy steered her old Honda into a parking spot, braking to a sudden stop. Her chest jerked against the seat belt, which pushed her backward so that her head thudded against the headrest. Standing beneath a leafless tree in front of the door to the church office, Janice Fontaine uncrossed her arms long enough to lower her sunglasses and look over the frame rim at her daughter. She shook her head, lips tight and drawn together, then pushed the glasses back into position and recrossed her arms.

Izzy smiled through the windshield, but on the inside she scolded herself. She shouldn't have taken the time to go to the Y. All the relaxation she'd felt after moving and stretching in the water was gone now, her muscles stiffening under Janice's displeased stare. Izzy pulled back her now dry hair and secured it with the ponytail holder she'd kept around her wrist. Just once, it would be nice if Mom would cut her some slack. Especially at a time like this.

Snatching the file folder from the passenger seat, Izzy left the car and walked toward her mother.

"Hi, Mom."

"Let me guess. You've just come from the pool." That was it. No preamble. No greeting. Just the accusation.

Izzy nodded her head, fingers tightening on the edge of the folder. "I did."

"If I'd known you were so drawn to swimming, I wouldn't have wasted all that money on dance lessons when you were younger." Janice looked in Izzy's direction, and though she couldn't see her mother's eyes behind the smoked lenses of her glasses, Izzy was certain she looked past her, not at her.

"You know why I swim," Izzy said. "It's good for me. It helps my joints."

Janice took a deep breath and her lips softened, the corners lowering and spreading out. "Yes, I know. I'm glad it helps you." She pointed at the folder. "What do you have in there?"

Before Izzy could say, she was cut off by the roar of a high-performance engine. Looking over her shoulder, she saw a sleek sports car zip through the parking lot. With a squeal of brakes it came to a stop right beside her ten-year-old vehicle.

Her brother sure knew how to make an entrance.

"Brandon!" The exuberance in Janice's voice left no doubt that she excused her eldest for his tardiness.

Izzy bit the inside of her lip as she watched her mother wrap her arms around her son. He was the favorite, without a doubt. Izzy had gotten to the point where she usually didn't let it bother her. But today was different. Today, the three of them were together because Gran had died. Izzy had been Gran's favorite, and vice versa. Watching her mother and brother interacting, knowing that Gran was gone, Izzy felt more alone than ever.

Brandon pulled away from their mother and put his arm around Izzy's shoulders. "How are you holding up, Tiny Dancer?"

The childhood nickname brought a smile to her lips. He hadn't called her that in years. "I'm OK. I miss her, though."

Janice smoothed down the front of her skirt. "Of course you do. We all do." She looked at the office door. "Now that we're all here, let's go in."

She took one step and wobbled on the uneven pavement. Brandon rushed forward and offered his arm. Izzy shook her head as she walked behind them. Why Janice insisted on wearing those ridiculous heels was beyond her. They had to be five inches, at least.

"Are those new shoes, Mom?" She knew better than to prod her mother, but she couldn't stop herself.

"Yes. And before you tell me I'm too old for shoes like this, don't. Do you know who I sold a pair of these to just yesterday?"

"Someone important, I'm sure."

Janice sniffed. "Only if you consider Meryl Streep important."

"Seriously?" Izzy asked. "Meryl Streep walked into your store?"

"Don't be silly," Janice said with a wave of her hand. "Meryl doesn't do her own shopping. But her assistant came in and bought a pair."

"Huh." The more Izzy heard, the less she thought her mother had all the facts. "So she came right out and told you she was Meryl Streep's assistant?"

"No. But when she bought them, she said, 'Meryl will love these'."

40

Brandon chuckled. "You know, there are other women in the world named Meryl."

Janice shook her head. "Not in Hollywood."

Izzy opened her mouth to argue that it was much more likely the assistant to someone named Meryl just needed a new pair of shoes for herself. But the look Brandon gave over his shoulder shut her down. He was right. Janice considered it a point of pride that, although she hadn't made it in Hollywood as an actress, she at least worked at an upscale boutique that catered to actresses. And their assistants. It would be a waste of time to point out that she spent entirely too much of her paycheck trying to emulate women thirty years her junior.

Thanks to her own sensible tennis shoes, Izzy jogged ahead of her mother and brother, grabbed the office door, and held it open for them. Since it was after regular office hours, Pastor Quaid greeted them by his secretary's desk.

"Izzy, so good to see you." He opened his beefy arms and she walked into his welcome bear hug. "How are you holding up?"

So much better now, she thought. "I'm good. Happy for Gran; sad for me."

He stepped back and smiled down at her.

"Of course. This entire congregation feels her absence." He turned to Izzy's mother. "You must be Isabella's daughter."

She removed her sunglasses and held out her hand. "Janice."

"So nice to meet you, Janice." He grabbed her hand and pumped it in both of his. "I feel like I already know you. Isabella talked about you all the time."

A brief look of shock flitted across her eyes, one corner of her mouth lifting in a half-smile. "She did?"

"Yes. And I'd know you anywhere. You certainly take after your mother."

Izzy cringed as her mother yanked her hand away, not at all happy to be told she resembled an eighty-seven-year-old dead woman. Poor Pastor Quaid. He'd been doing so well up to that point.

"Pastor." Izzy spoke up, hoping to diffuse the tension. "This is my brother, Brandon."

He and Brandon shook hands and exchanged pleasantries without incident. Then Pastor Quaid turned back to Izzy. "If you're ready, we can go back to my office and talk about the service."

Pastor Quaid obviously deferred to her since she was a member of his church. But Izzy knew better than to take the lead now. There were certain things about the service she wanted to make sure happened, but it was best not to act like she was in charge. It was a matter of choosing her battles, something Izzy was extremely familiar with.

"Mom." Izzy turned to her. "Are you ready?"

Janice nodded. Pastor Quaid turned and led the way down the hall. Janice crooked her elbow so Brandon could thread his arm back through and offer support. They followed, looking like they were leaning on each other.

Izzy took up the rear. Alone.

4

"You can't be serious." Janice perched on the edge of her chair, looking at Izzy as though her daughter had lost her mind. "This is a funeral, not Mardi Gras."

Hands clasped tightly in her lap, Izzy was determined not to lose her cool. " 'When the Saints Go Marching In' was Gran's favorite song. She'd want us to sing it."

"Oh, and you know that for a fact."

"Yes, I do."

"How?"

"She told me."

Janice's verbal assault came to a halt. She looked at Brandon, who shrugged. Then she looked back at Izzy, ignoring the pastor as she had through most of the meeting. "She told you what music she wanted at her funeral? That's so morbid."

"It's only morbid if you think of death as the end of everything, but Isabella didn't." Pastor Quaid's deep voice commanded the attention of everyone in the room, even Janice. "Isabella knew that death was the beginning of her real life. Her eternal life. That's why she wanted her funeral to be a celebration."

Janice frowned. "It's just not dignified."

Izzy looked down, catching a glimpse of her mother's oh-so-unsensible shoes. The woman had an odd idea of what was dignified.

Now Brandon leaned toward Janice, and the folding chair that Pastor Quaid had brought in for extra seating creaked beneath him. "What difference does it make what we sing? Let's just do what Gran wanted."

"That's just the thing. I don't know what she wanted." Janice's hands fluttered in front of her as if trying to clear away a fog too thick to see through. "I don't even know why I'm here."

Izzy reached out and grabbed her mother's hand. "You're here because you loved her and she loved you. But if this is too much for you, I can take care of it."

For the first time since they'd arrived, Janice looked at Izzy with something other than disdain or disapproval. "Really? You'd do that?"

"Of course. I just don't want you to feel left out." Izzy knew she was taking a chance by offering to take over. When they arrived the next afternoon for the service, anything Mom didn't like would be Izzy's fault. But it was a chance she was willing to take.

Janice stood up so quickly that her purse fell from her lap and landed beside the chair with a thud. "Thank you. Thank you so much." In an uncharacteristic display of affection, she sandwiched Izzy's cheeks between her palms and kissed her on the forehead.

"You're welcome," Izzy mumbled through compressed lips.

Brandon scooped up Janice's purse as he stood, and looked at Izzy. "Since you've got this covered, I think I should take her home."

"What about my car?" Janice asked.

"We'll get it tomorrow." He turned toward Pastor Quaid. "It'll be safe here, right?"

"Absolutely."

Janice gave her son a tender smile. "You're so sweet to think of that. Let's go, then."

Brandon winked at Izzy before following his mother to the door. Izzy wasn't sure if it was a conspiratorial gesture between siblings or a way to gloat that he'd gotten out of the meeting, too. Either way, she was relieved to see them both go.

As he opened the door for her, Janice said,

"This has me so stressed out. I need to find a way to relax tonight. Maybe I'll watch a movie on Netflix."

Izzy nearly suggested *Sunset Boulevard,* but pressed her lips together against the impulse. Once the door shut behind them, she leaned forward, head in her hands, and let out a groan.

Behind his desk, Pastor Quaid laughed. "Are you sure you're related to them?"

"Sometimes I wonder." Taking a deep breath, she closed her eyes and counted to five. Maybe now she and the pastor could make some forward movement. When she looked back at him, he was smiling. "What?"

"You looked so much like your grandmother when you did that. Which reminds me . . ." He held up a finger then leaned over and pulled open the bottom drawer of his desk. When he sat back up, he had a small box in his hand. "This is for you."

Izzy smiled as she took it. "Thanks. But you didn't need to do this."

"I didn't. It's from Isabella."

She almost dropped the box. "From Gran? When did she give it to you?"

"Before she moved into the assisted living facility. She made me promise not to give it to you until after her death. The last time I saw her, she reminded me about it. Between

47

you and me, I think she knew her time was coming."

Izzy nodded in agreement, only half listening to what the man said. Turning the box over in her hand, she studied its plain brown wrapper tied with coarse yellow string. First the quilt, now this. Not only did Gran want her passing to be a celebration, she was turning it into a crazy backward scavenger hunt as well.

"Izzy, are you all right?"

She looked up at Pastor Quaid. His voice was gentle; his eyes brimming with genuine concern. A pang zinged Izzy's heart. If her father were still alive, she imagined he'd be a lot like her pastor. And if Dad were still alive, Mom would be a totally different woman.

She sniffed and dabbed the corner of one eye with her knuckle. "I'm fine. Just the thought that Gran wanted to make sure I had this . . . well, it got to me."

"I understand. Would you like some time alone to open it?"

"No. I'll open it later." She and her dysfunctional family had taken up enough of the pastor's evening. He had a perfectly well-functioning family of his own to get home to. "Let's get back to the arrangements for tomorrow."

If Mom was irked about ending the service with "When the Saints Go Marching In," Izzy doubted she'd be happy about the Christmas carols they'd be singing. But at that moment, Izzy didn't care.

Gran wanted a party, and a party she would get.

Izzy frowned at herself in the mirror. She looked as if she were going to a funeral. Mom would be pleased, but Gran would hate it.

"What do you think, Bogie?" She glanced at a pile of clothes on the floor by her dresser, then grabbed a bright blue scarf that was draped around one of the tall bedposts. "Can I get away with a splash of color?"

The pile of clothes shuddered as the terrier poked his nose out from under her discarded pajama bottoms. He looked up at her, cocked his head, and barked once.

"I agree," she said with a nod to her reflection. She folded the soft fabric in half, draped it around her neck, and pulled the two ends through the open loop. Then she fluffed and arranged the material until it had just the look of casual elegance she had hoped for. "Much better." Gran would be proud.

Gran's voice spoke in her head, clear as day. *Of course I'd be proud. I've always been your biggest fan.*

Izzy stooped down to pull the clothes off Bogie and tossed them on top of her bed. Taking his wire-haired little head between her hands, she looked into his melted-chocolate eyes. "We're saying our final good-byes to Gran today. It's just you and me now, buddy."

He pushed his nose forward and tried to lick her face, but she was too fast for him. There would be time for cuddling later, after the service was over and it didn't matter that he shed white fur all over her black dress. For now, she had to remain as presentable as she could.

As she stood up, her eyes fell on the small brown box sitting on her nightstand. She'd been so tired by the time she got home last night, she had decided not to open the present. Instead, she'd wait and open it before the funeral. But now, looking at her last gift from Gran, she wondered if maybe it would be better to open it after she said her good-byes.

A car horn blew outside, making the decision for her. "That's my brother," she said to the dog. "Are you a praying man, Bogie? If not, this would be a good time to start."

She dashed from her bedroom and headed out of the house, grabbing her purse along the way. Once outside, she pulled the front door shut, locked it, then turned. And froze on the porch.

When Brandon called that morning suggesting he pick up both their mother and her, it had seemed like a good idea. That way, in the highly likely event that Mom still wasn't up to driving home the car she'd left at church, Izzy could do it. Besides that, she liked the thought of the three of them arriving at church together, like a normal family would. It all made sense.

It also made sense that Brandon, who owned three cars, would choose one that could comfortably accommodate three people.

But when had her big brother ever done anything that made sense?

The Mini Cooper in her driveway was cherry red, sleek, and had a roomy backseat — if you were a two-year-old.

As she stared, Brandon opened his door and unfolded his tall frame, resting his forearms on the roof. "Are you going to get in the car or stand there all day?"

She walked up to the vehicle, noting that her mother already held court in the passenger seat. When she got to Brandon's side, he reached down and pulled the driver's seat forward. Izzy lifted one foot, then stopped.

"Now what?" Brandon huffed in irritation.

"I'm just trying to figure out how to get in." Crawling into the small space behind the front seat was always a challenge, but doing it while wearing heels and a skirt turned it into a perilous act.

"Isabella, quit fooling around and get in the car."

Mom's command, combined with the use of her formal first name, snapped Izzy as if she'd shot it from a rubber-band gun. When Izzy was little, she couldn't understand why she and her grandmother had the same name. Mom got tired of answering the same questions over and over, so instead she called her Izzy. Now that Gran was gone, Mom must have thought it was OK to go back to the old name again.

Izzy looked at Brandon. His thumb tapped restlessly on the black leather of the seat. "You should have brought a bigger car." She whispered the words, hoping her mother wouldn't hear.

He looked down at her skirt and shoes, and the thumb tapping stopped. "I'm sorry, Iz. I brought the Coop because Mom loves it. I didn't even think about how small the back is."

Of course he didn't. Because Brandon lived his life that way, jumping from impulse to impulse, doing what his gut told him to do. Somehow, it worked for him. His bold risk-taking had made him a bundle in business. But a person couldn't be right all the time. What worried Izzy was that one day, his gut would send him in the wrong direction.

But today wasn't the right time to think about Brandon and his life choices. Today was about Gran's life: the mortal life she had lived and the eternal one she was living right now.

"It's OK, Brandon." Izzy smiled. "But can you help me get in?"

Her brother clasped her hand in his. As he helped her maneuver her way into the cramped space, his palm on the small of her back, her mind flashed to the time when she was six, learning to ride her new bike. Dad had taken off the training wheels. He and Brandon stood on either side of the bike, holding it steady, jogging down the street with her as she pedaled, her knees pumping faster and faster. When they let go, Mom laughed and clapped, doing a little hop on the front lawn.

Izzy had one foot in the car, but as she brought her other foot in, the toe of her shoe caught on the door frame and she lost her balance. With a little grunt and a final push from Brandon, Izzy dropped onto the car seat. She looked up at her mother, hoping to see a trace of the happy, exuberant woman from her memory. No such luck. That woman had been gone for a long time.

5

The church was half full by the time they arrived. As they made their way from the parking lot to the sanctuary, Izzy was stopped more than once by folk who wanted to wish her well and share their condolences.

"I didn't know Gran had so many friends." Brandon kept his voice low as he walked between his mother and Izzy.

Mom nodded. "Your grandmother always was the life of the party." She looked like she had more to say, but she pressed her lips together and swallowed, her eyelashes fluttering.

A lifetime of reading her mother's body language told Izzy they needed to get her into the church and sitting down before she fell apart. "Brandon, why don't you and Mom go in? There's a pew reserved for family right up front."

"Where are you going?" he asked.

"I need to find Pastor Quaid. Let him

know we're here and make sure everything's ready."

Brandon frowned. "OK. But don't take too long."

She watched them walk away. Mom was once again hanging on to his arm like a drowning woman clutching driftwood, but this time her shoes weren't totally to blame. Mom and Gran had had a rocky relationship, but they still loved each other. No daughter could lose her mother and not need some support.

Izzy took a deep breath just as Edna Summers, the church organist, approached her.

"Sweetheart, I am so sorry for your loss." She took Izzy's hands in hers and squeezed them tight. Edna was a little bird of a woman, but years of pressing the keys of the pipe organ had kept her fingers nimble and strong.

"Thank you. And thank you for playing today."

"My pleasure, dear. I love everything you picked. I'm sure Isabella will be looking down from her heavenly perch, singing along and dancing in the aisles."

The image made Izzy smile. "I bet you're right. Have you seen Pastor Quaid? I want to talk to him before the service starts."

Edna motioned behind her. "Try his office. He's probably getting in some quiet prayer time."

Izzy hugged the woman, then headed toward the back of the building. Rounding a corner, she ran right into a tall man in a navy blue suit. As his hands reached out to steady her, she looked up — not at the man she was looking for, but into the eyes of the last man she expected to see that day.

"You've got to be kidding," she growled.

Max Logan's brow furrowed. "Excuse me?"

She took a step backward, hands up and palms facing him. "What's the deal with you? You can't take no for an answer so now you're following me to my grandmother's funeral?"

"Miss, you've got the wrong idea. I —"

"No, you've got the wrong idea." She jabbed a finger at him. "My grandmother is dead. The last thing I want to do is talk to you about a smelly, raggedy old quilt!"

Color rose in Max's cheeks, and a muscle twitched in his jaw. "You might want to keep your voice down. People are starting to look."

Making a scene wouldn't honor Gran's memory, but she wasn't about to let him off the hook, either. "Please leave," she said, her voice low and well mannered.

"I can't do that," he answered, equally as calm.

"Why not?"

"Because I'm here with my grandfather."

Izzy's stomach dropped as she realized the mistake she'd made. "You brought Virgil?"

"Yes. To pay our respects. Not to talk about the heirloom quilt you have so little respect for."

She couldn't even look at him. Her eyes burned as she dropped her gaze to the pavement. "I'm sorry. I had no right to attack you like that. It's just been so hard since Gran died, and I've been at odds with my brother and my mother, and . . . and . . ."

Izzy never cried in front of people. Ever. But to her horror, she was crying now. That one small confession to a man she barely knew blew a hole through her emotional dam and everything she'd held back for the last week flooded out. When he put his hand on her arm, she cried harder. And when he pulled her down the pathway, she stumbled along with him, blind to where they were going.

"Sit down."

As he guided her onto a wood and wrought-iron bench, Izzy realized they were in the area set aside as a prayer garden. In the summer months, it was a beautiful place to be, full of bright, colorful flowers and lush green plants. Now, it was brown and withered, a perfect complement to her battered spirit. A moment later, Max pressed a white handkerchief into her palm. She looked down at it, and a laugh mixed with her tears.

"How many of these things do you have?"

"A stockpile. My mother taught me that a gentleman always carries a handkerchief."

Izzy nodded and dabbed at her eyes. When she looked at the white cotton, now streaked with black mascara residue, she gasped. "I'm afraid I just ruined it."

He shrugged. "That's OK. Consider it a peace offering."

Peace. What a lovely idea. There'd been more than enough conflict in Izzy's life already; she didn't need any more. On Monday, she and Max would once again be at cross-purposes, but for today, they could be civil.

"Thanks. I'd like that." She continued dabbing at her eyes, but Max shook his head and took the handkerchief from her.

"Don't take this the wrong way, but you're just making it worse." He found a clean spot on the fabric and wrapped it around his finger. "Close your eyes."

She leaned away from him.

He laughed. "It's OK. I'm a gentleman, remember? And we're in the middle of a truce. You can trust me."

She let her lids fall, exhaling a deep breath. A moment later, his soft, cotton-covered fingertip swept across the skin at the top of her cheek. When it rubbed a bit harder, her head jerked away.

"Hold still. I don't want to poke you in the eye." His murmured words were followed by the warm fingers of his free hand embracing her jawline and chin, holding her head steady.

As Max tended to makeup repair, Izzy began to relax. For a moment, she let herself forget all the things that had gone wrong in the last week and simply concentrated on the luxury of being taken care of. A smile grew on her lips, and a thumb brushed across the corner of her mouth.

Izzy's eyelids snapped up. Max had finished cleaning off her errant mascara, but his hand still rested against her cheek. His eyes, brown and bottomless, looked as surprised as she felt.

"Why are you being so nice to me?" Izzy's voice crackled in her throat.

Before Max could respond, a voice called out to them. "There you are!"

Max's hand jerked away as if he'd touched

a hot stove. He turned toward Virgil, who was shuffling down the path toward them. "Izzy needed some time alone before the service."

Virgil put his hand on his grandson's shoulder and looked down at Izzy. "I see. I'm glad Max could be there for you when you needed to be alone."

The way his eyes danced, Izzy was certain he'd seen Max touching her cheek. She cleared her throat and smiled. "I'm feeling much better now. And thanks to your grandson, I no longer look like a raccoon. Now I really need to find Pastor Quaid before the service starts."

As Izzy stood up, her left knee caught. *Not now.* Whether it was from the damp November weather or the build-up of stress, her body was not doing well. She flexed her leg until the joint gave way, returning to somewhat fluid movement. But when she stepped forward, it wasn't as steady as she had hoped.

Max wrapped his hand around her forearm, steadying her. "You know, I would sure appreciate it if you'd take Virgil in and show him where to sit. He's looking a bit tired."

Virgil's eyebrows shot up like two bushy white exclamation points. "Why, I'm not —" The two men's eyes locked and Virgil

61

nodded his head. "I'm not feeling as perky as I thought I was. It would be nice to sit down for a while."

Izzy bit her lip. What a pair these two were. She barely knew them but they looked out for her welfare like she was part of their family. "I still need to talk to Pastor Quaid."

"I'll find him for you." Max said. "If he needs anything, I'll come get you. OK?"

"OK." Izzy nodded. She crooked her arm through Virgil's and, just like her mother and brother before them, they held each other up.

As they exited the garden, Izzy glanced over her shoulder. Max still stood by the bench, hands stuffed in his pants pockets, watching them.

Max couldn't stop watching her.

After finding Pastor Quaid and getting his assurance that everything was running smoothly, he'd gone to the sanctuary in search of Virgil. He'd found him directly behind the row reserved for family.

"Why did you sit so close to the front?" Max whispered as he slid in beside him.

"Izzy put me here. Guess that makes us family."

Not quite. But it meant she realized how important his grandfather had been to her grandmother. And maybe that the two families could continue being important to each other.

Izzy sat on the end of the row. Beside her was a man whose tailored black suit had certainly cost more than all the clothes in Max's closet combined. His arm was slung over the back of the pew and he leaned toward her, whispering in her ear. Max's spine stiffened. Was he her boyfriend? Or part of the family?

On the other side of the man, a woman brought her hand to her mouth, stifling a sob, but not before it got the man's attention. He immediately turned from Izzy and took up the same posture with this woman. "Are you OK, Mom?"

Mom. It was the family pew, so if this woman was his mother, it stood to reason she was Izzy's mother also. Which made the man Izzy's brother. Max enjoyed a moment of relief. Then he asked himself why it mattered to him whether or not Izzy had a boyfriend.

He had no answer.

Max tried to concentrate on the service, on the celebration of the life of Isabella Randolph, but it was useless. His thoughts kept going back to Izzy, and he couldn't keep his eyes off her. When they first met, he'd wondered if she was a student, but he couldn't make that mistake today. Her hair hung loose around her shoulders, cascading in a silky golden waterfall over the bright blue scarf that broke up the somberness of her black dress. From where he sat he could hear the triumph in her voice as they sang "Joy to the World." When the pastor told a humorous story about her grandmother, Izzy's full-throated laughter drew a laugh from Max as well.

An elbow caught him in the ribs. He turned to Virgil, who leaned over and hissed at him. "Don't make it so obvious, son."

Max wanted to correct his grandfather, tell him he'd misunderstood, but he couldn't. Gramps had caught him red-handed. What was he doing? It wasn't like him to lose his head over a woman, no matter how attractive she was. And to be fawning over her at her grandmother's funeral . . . definitely not the act of a gentleman. He needed to pay attention to what the pastor was saying and not let his focus drift.

The man in the pulpit smiled down at the friends and family in the pews. "Isabella didn't have a perfect life, but she never lost the joy that comes with knowing who you are in Jesus — something she shared with her namesake granddaughter, whom we all know as Izzy." He leaned on the highly varnished wood in front of him, craning his neck and smiling down on her. "Izzy, you inherited more than her name. Even today, when our hearts are heavy, I see the same joy in you. You are her legacy."

Every eye in the church turned toward Izzy, so Max had no choice but to follow suit. She had been doing a good job holding herself together, but Pastor Quaid's tender words undermined her composure. She sniffled, trying to hold the tears back. Head down, shoulders shaking, she struggled. Max looked at her brother, glaring at the back of his head and mentally demanding that he offer comfort.

Her brother removed his arm from their mother's shoulders and leaned toward his sister. But before he could put a consoling hand on her knee, the mother let loose with a series of gut-wrenching sobs. The son paused for a split second, unsure who needed his attention more, but his mother won out.

Max leaned forward in his seat. He wanted to console Izzy. He wanted to gather her up in his arms and let her cry all over the front of his jacket, runny mascara or not. But he couldn't. He wasn't family. He wasn't even a friend. He was barely an acquaintance.

65

He'd overstepped enough already.

Virgil didn't let lack of familiarity stop him. He pulled himself up, walked to Izzy, and plunked down on the hard wooden seat, wedging himself between her and the side of the pew. As soon as he put his arm around her shoulders, she leaned into him, letting her tears silently fall onto the lapel of his sport coat.

Letting out a sigh, Max leaned back as the tension fell from his shoulders. Thank God for Gramps. Nobody would think twice about a grandfather figure lending a shoulder. If only Max could stop wishing it was *his* shoulder she was pressed against.

It didn't take long for Izzy to regain her composure. When the organist pounded out a rousing rendition of "When the Saints Go Marching In," Izzy was on her feet, clapping and smiling. There was that joy the pastor mentioned. She certainly had it in abundance.

As the last notes died down, Pastor Quaid addressed the crowd again. "The Fontaine family would like to thank you for celebrating Isabella's homecoming. Anyone who'd like to join them at the cemetery for the interment is welcome. Otherwise, please enjoy cookies and punch in the multipurpose room."

Izzy turned to her brother. "I'll meet you and Mom at the cemetery."

Brandon looked up from his seat in the pew. He still had one arm around the shoulders of his mother, who was doubled over, a fistful of used tissues clenched to her nose. "Why aren't you coming with us?"

"I've got to drive her car, remember?"

"That's right." He frowned and looked from his sister to his mother and back again. "Will you be OK by yourself?"

Izzy nodded and smiled at him. But as Brandon led their mother away, Max noticed the quiver in Izzy's chin as she forced that smile to stay in place. He couldn't keep his mouth shut any longer.

"You really shouldn't be alone right now," he said, getting as close to her as the pew between them would allow.

For a moment, he thought she was going to argue the point. But then her mouth relaxed and she blinked several times. "You know, I don't *want* to be alone, either. Were you two planning to come to the cemetery?"

"No," Max said.

"Yes," Virgil said a split second later.

"Yes." Max amended his answer as the skin around his collar darkened a few shades. "I guess we are."

Izzy smiled again, only this time it was

real. "Good."

"And I'll ride with you," Virgil offered. "To keep you company."

Izzy nodded and they left the church together. It took a good fifteen minutes to get to the parking lot, what with all the folk that stopped Izzy for hugs and handshakes. Max kept his eye on her, looking for any signs that she was overwhelmed, but her spirits seemed to rise the more people she talked to. He finally relaxed when they reached their cars.

He was glad Izzy had someone traveling with her. Not that Virgil could offer more than moral support. He hadn't had a driver's license in years, and he just recently learned how to make calls on his in-case-of-emergencies cell phone. But Max drove right behind them, his eyes pinned on Izzy.

Just as they had been all day long.

6

The doors to the emergency room waiting area barely had time to slide open as Izzy ran between them, turning sideways to squeeze through the small opening.

"My mother was just brought in," she said to the nurse behind the counter. "We were at the cemetery and she twisted her ankle and fell down some stairs."

The woman looked up from her computer monitor. "What's your mother's name?"

"Janice. Janice Fontaine."

"Just one moment."

As the nurse's fingernails clicked on the keyboard, two phrases chased each other in Izzy's head — the same two phrases that had been circling for the last half hour: *Please God, let her be all right* and *Why did she wear those stupid shoes?*

Izzy jumped as a hand squeezed her shoulder. Max stood beside her.

"What's the word?"

"I don't know yet. The nurse is checking." Izzy glanced behind him. "Where's Virgil?"

"Over there." He pointed to a bank of vending machines across the room. "I told him to get himself a snack."

"Here we go." Izzy and Max turned their attention back to the nurse. "They're checking her out right now."

"Can I see her?" Izzy asked.

"Sorry," she shook her head. "She already has a visitor, and only one's allowed in the emergency area."

Of course Brandon and his zippy sports car had made it there first. "OK. Can you at least tell me how she is?"

"All I can tell you is that they're taking her to X-ray. Have a seat and I'll let you know as soon as I have more information."

Izzy moved into the waiting area and settled on a hard, vinyl-upholstered chair against the wall. Max sat beside her. A moment later, Virgil joined them.

"Look what I found in the snack machine. A Mallo Cup." He sat on the other side of Izzy and unwrapped his candy. "I haven't seen one of these since 1972."

"That's probably how long it's been in the machine," Max answered.

As the two of them discussed the longevity of sugar-based products, Izzy stared down at her clasped hands. Worry warred with guilt as she recalled the accident at the cemetery. She'd seen her mother stumble and trip. Seen her arms flailing, seeking but not finding something solid to hold on to. Seen her roll down six steps and thud to a stop at the bottom, momentarily silent until she let loose with a cry of true, genuine pain. Still, Izzy couldn't keep herself from thinking that on this day when they were all supposed to be focused on Gran, Mom had found a way to put herself back in the spotlight.

It was a terrible thing to think. What kind of a daughter would suspect such a thing? Mom was a master at bringing attention back around to her, but even she wouldn't purposely take a header down a flight of concrete stairs. Would she?

Izzy sighed, and Virgil immediately patted her knee.

"Your mother is going to be fine," he said. "You just need to stop worrying."

"How can I? It's all I can think about."

"Then we need to make you think about something else." He leaned forward and looked across her at his grandson. "Tell her about yourself, Max."

"Excuse me?" Max frowned at Virgil.

"Well, sure. You're an interesting young

man. You must have some stories to tell."

"Nothing like yours. Why don't you tell her one of your stories?"

"Because I'm old. She'll be more interested in you."

"Fellas." Izzy laughed and held up her hands. "No need to fight over who's not going to tell me a story. I'm fine. Really." She turned toward Max. "But since we've got some time to kill, we might as well talk about the quilt."

"Really?" His eyebrows rose in surprise. "Here?"

"Why not?"

"OK." Max looked over at Virgil, then back at Izzy. "I'm not sure where to start."

Izzy leaned back in the chair. She didn't know where they should start, either. "You said Gran promised the quilt to you. It might help me to know why you were interested in it in the first place."

"I'm putting together a new exhibit at the museum and that quilt is the focal point."

Izzy sighed. For some reason, Max seemed to only want to dole out small bits of information. It could take forever to get to the bottom of this. "OK, so you need a quilt as part of your exhibit. But why Gran's quilt? What makes it so special?"

"The provenance."

"Provenance is the backstory of a piece," Virgil said, gently tapping her shoulder.

Izzy glanced at him and smiled. After years of watching *Antiques Roadshow* on PBS, she was familiar with provenance, but she was happy to let him think he'd just taught her something new.

"Well, I'm at a disadvantage," she said, looking back to Max. "Because other than the fact that it's a Wild Goose Chase pattern, I don't know anything about the quilt."

"It's pretty amazing. According to Isabella, the quilt was started by one of her relatives back in the 1800s. Over the years, it was passed down from one woman to the next until it was completed."

"You mean one woman didn't sew the entire quilt?"

Max shook his head. "No. Remember, the quilting was done by hand, so it took a while. As a rule, the material was hard to come by. It was a fairly common practice for quilts to be passed down from one generation to the next until they were finished." Max leaned closer now, his eyes wide, a grin lifting one corner of his mouth. "What's special about this quilt is that it was started in Vermont and it ended up in California. It was worked on by the very pioneer women who helped settle our nation. If that quilt could talk, imagine the stories it could tell."

If that quilt could talk, maybe it could tell Izzy why Gran never told her about it. That part still made no sense. But then, neither did so many of the events of the last week.

"That's great, but surely it's not the only quilt to be brought across country."

Max's brows scrunched together, as if he were trying to process what she'd just said. "No, I'm sure it's not. But it's one of the few to have documentation."

"Documentation?"

Virgil tapped her shoulder again. "That's —"

"I know what it is," she said, not feeling the need to indulge him for a second time. "I'm not sure what kind of documentation you're talking about."

Now the trace of Max's grin vanished. "Mrs. Randolph said she had diaries that belonged to the women who made the quilt. Don't you have them?"

Izzy shook her head slowly. "Not that I know of. It's possible Gran could have them in the house somewhere, but I don't know where."

"It's very important that you find them." Max reached out and his fingers closed around her wrist. His grip was firm, not enough to hurt her, but enough that she knew he was serious. "They're just as valuable as the quilt."

"What's valuable?"

Brandon's voice broke into their conversation and Izzy looked up to see her brother walking across the room, his suit jacket slung over one arm. She jumped to her feet. "How's Mom?"

"Pretty beat up." He rubbed the back of his neck with his free hand. "She broke her leg and dislocated her shoulder. She'll be in pain for a while, but she's going to be all right."

"When can we take her home?"

"Not until tomorrow. She's got a bruise on her head, so they're keeping her overnight for observation. Just to be sure. But when they do release her . . . uh . . ." He took a deep breath then blew it out with force. "She's going to have to move in with you."

"What?" Izzy took a step back and ran her calf into the chair.

"It's just temporary," Brandon rushed on, waving his palm at her. "She can barely walk and she's got a bum arm. There's no way she can stay by herself."

"Can't she stay with you?"

"My condo's two stories and the bathroom is on the second floor, remember? Lots of stairs and no elevator. I'm afraid she's all yours, Sis."

There was no use fighting it. Brandon was right. His place was totally out of the question. Mom would have to stay with her while she healed up.

Izzy heard a grunt and a snuffle. Behind her, Virgil dozed in his chair. She turned to Max. "You should probably get him home."

Max stood up. "Are you going to be all right?"

"Yes. I can't tell you how much I appreciate your support today."

"I'm sorry," her brother blurted out. "We haven't met. I'm Brandon Fontaine. Izzy's brother."

"Max Logan." He held out his hand, making Brandon shift his coat from one arm to the other in order to reciprocate. "This is my grandfather, Virgil. We were friends of Mrs. Randolph. And now, of Izzy."

"I see." Brandon pumped his hand, sizing him up. "Well, thanks for staying with my sister. But I've got it from here."

"Good to hear." Max moved to Virgil and shook him gently. "Gramps. It's time to go."

"Huh? What?" Virgil looked around, eyelids half-open. "I didn't miss dinner, did I? It's tapioca night."

"Don't worry. I'll get you back in time for tapioca." Max looked at Izzy. "Will I see you on Monday?"

She nodded. "Absolutely. Four o'clock at the museum."

As the two men walked away, Izzy again took note of how Max cared for his grandfather. In the same way, he'd cared for her today, even though they barely knew each other. If his mother had set out to raise a gentleman, she'd certainly done a fine job of it.

"You have a date on Monday?" Brandon asked.

"It's not a date. It's a business meeting."

"At a museum?"

"Yes."

Brandon tilted his head, just a bit. "A meeting at a museum about something valuable? Sounds interesting."

Izzy sighed. Why did her brother always see dollar signs before anything else? "I'll tell you about it later. Can I go back and see Mom now?"

"Sure. She's been asking for you."

"She has?"

"Yeah, she's already making a list of the things she needs you to get from her house."

Oh goody. They left the waiting room and headed to a bank of elevators. "Did the doctor say how long it will take her to heal?"

"About eight weeks, give or take."

Brandon threw it out casually, like it was no time at all. But Izzy immediately did the math. Eight weeks. Two months. *If* Mom behaved herself, which was a very big *if*. Which meant Mom would be staying with her through Thanksgiving, Christmas, and into the new year.

Tidings of comfort and joy would be a lot harder to come by this holiday season.

7

"It's just me, Bogie."

Izzy maneuvered past the dog and into the house, pushing the heavy door closed behind her with her foot. Bogie stopped barking but he pranced around her feet, his nose pointed at the fast-food bag dangling from her hand.

"This isn't for you."

The scolding sent him slinking into the corner. He lay down, nose on paws, but kept his eyes trained on her.

Depositing her armload of stuff on the table, Izzy let out a sigh. "What a day." She kicked off her shoes and stretched out her poor, tired feet. As a rule, Izzy avoided heels. Even the sensible ones she'd chosen today threw her body out of whack if she wore them too long. And everything about today had gone on too long.

A few minutes later, dressed in her most comfortable pair of sweatpants and a baggy sweatshirt, Izzy curled up on the couch with her fast-food dinner. As she was about to take a bite of her burger, Bogie whimpered.

Izzy shook her head. How could that one little sound communicate so much? "OK. You can join me." The dog shot up as if on springs, scampered over, and jumped onto the couch. Izzy held up her palm, giving him the signal to sit and stay. "You know the rules, buddy. You have your side; I have mine."

Bogie sat, head up, giving her his full attention. Either that or he was thinking of a way to abscond with her bag of fries.

Izzy took a bite of her burger. She chewed slowly, savoring not just the food but the silence around her. One of the things she loved most about this house was its sense of calm and peace. She used to think it came from Gran, but even after Gran moved into Vibrant Vistas the serene atmosphere remained. How long would it last once Janice Fontaine moved in?

Izzy swallowed and the once delicious mouthful hit the bottom of her stomach like a rock. She forced herself to finish half the burger and nibble on a few fries but her appetite had been mostly chased away by the thought of how her life was about to change.

She tossed a fry to Bogie, who seemed to

catch, chew, and swallow it all in one motion. Then she crumpled the bag around the remaining food, took it in the kitchen, and tossed it in the trash. What would Mom say when she got here? She hadn't been to the house since last Thanksgiving. Walking back to the living room, Izzy took in the curio cabinet of knickknacks, the pictures on the walls, and the furniture that had been in the family for generations. All of it would be a daily reminder to her mother that Gran had chosen to hand down the house to Izzy.

This was not a good situation.

Flopping down on the couch, Izzy looked at the dog. "Brace yourself. My mother is moving in with us for a few months."

If they were living in a sitcom, Bogie would have jumped from the couch and dashed from the room. At the very least, he would have stuck his head under a cushion. But since it was real life, he yawned and lay down, completely uninterested in anything she had to say now that the food had disappeared.

"I wish I could be so relaxed."

What she really wished, more than anything, was that Gran was still with her. But Gran was gone, and she'd left a bunch of questions and cryptic gifts in her place.

Gifts.

Izzy got to her feet, teetered for a moment, and then headed for the bedroom. There it was on her nightstand, the box Pastor Quaid had given her.

"What other surprises have you got for me, Gran?"

Sitting cross-legged on her mattress, Izzy undid the twine bow and lifted the top off the box. There was a note inside. She put the box on her pillow, unfolded the paper, and began to read.

My sweet Isabella,

If you're reading this now, that means I'm gone.

Izzy couldn't help but laugh. It was the same line she'd started the other note with. Gran must have stolen it from a movie or book in which a dying woman left gifts behind for her loved ones. Admonishing herself to be serious, she kept reading.

Very soon, you'll be contacted by Virgil, a dear friend of mine. He has a very special gift for you. I trust Virgil implicitly, and you can too.

Obviously, Gran underestimated how seriously Virgil took his position as guardian of the quilt and expected Pastor Quaid to get to Izzy first.

Your mother and brother will want to see my will, but there isn't one. I did that on purpose.

Initially, this will cause contention, but my hope is that, in the long run, it will bring our family back together. But it can only happen if you are the peacemaker. Isabella, you are stronger than you know, and God's love abides in you. No matter how difficult things get, you are never alone.

You may wonder why I'm being so mysterious. Let me just say that some things are better learned than told. Some truths mean more when they are lived than explained. Live the truth, Isabella, and it will lead you to a treasure greater than anything you could imagine.

She signed it, *All my love, Gran.*

Izzy sniffed and wiped the tears from her cheeks with the cuff of her sweatshirt. Where were Max and his handkerchiefs when she needed them?

The clicking of toenails announced that Bogie was coming into the room. He stood at her feet, head cocked to one side, eyes gazing up at her. The four-poster bed was too high for him to jump onto by himself, so she reached down and scooped him up with her free hand.

"You're a sweetie. Even if you only love me because I give you treats." As she hugged him to her side, she set down the note and picked up the box from her pillow. Several layers of light pink tissue paper were carefully folded, covering something. She looked at Bogie. "I'm almost afraid to see what's under there."

The dog lifted his nose as if trying to see what she was holding, and kneaded her thigh with his paws.

"OK, OK. I'll look."

Carefully, as though the tissue might fall to pieces in her hands, she peeled back each sheet of paper until she revealed another bit of wrapping.

A piece of white seersucker with bold stripes of pink, yellow, and green was wrapped around something small and hard. Unfolding the fabric, she found it was cut in the shape of a triangle. She had barely noticed that it was the same shape as the pieces of the Wild Goose Chase quilt when the actual gift fell from it and plopped in her lap.

"Oh my."

It was Gran's favorite necklace. She lifted it up by the delicate chain, sending the pendant of three interlocked rings — one of clear stones, one of red, and another of green — swaying and sparkling.

When she was about ten, Izzy had asked her grandmother if the stones in the rings were real. They had been in the kitchen, making cookies. Gran answered without looking up from the batter she was stirring. "They might be diamonds, rubies, and emeralds. Or they might just be colored glass. What difference does it make? I love it because it reminds me of your grandfather." She'd rubbed the rings between her fingertips, and her eyes took on a far-off look. "Even though he's gone, in a way, he's always with me."

There was no note to explain why Gran had given her the necklace, but she didn't need one. Gran was always with her, and this was her way of making sure Izzy never forgot.

8

"This hospital food is terrible. Why would they give a chicken breast to someone with her arm in a sling?"

It had been nonstop complaints from Janice since Izzy arrived at the hospital, but she was trying very hard to be empathetic. She tried to imagine how much pain her mother must be in and how frustrated she must be. Watching her jab at her food with her left hand drove the point home.

"Let me help you with that, Mom."

Izzy took the fork, half expecting Janice to shoo her away, but she didn't.

"Thank you," she almost whispered.

"No problem." Izzy picked up the plastic knife and began sawing at the tough piece of chicken on the tray. It likely tasted just as bad as it looked. Maybe some chit-chat would distract her mother from her inedible lunch. "I put your name on the prayer list at church today."

Janice snorted. "Oh fine. Now everyone will know my business."

"Not everyone. Just the people who pray the most. And they'll keep it between themselves and God."

"Sure they will."

Izzy leaned forward, concentrating on cutting the chicken into bite-size pieces. Why did Mom care if anybody knew she'd fallen down and hurt herself? She didn't even know those people. You'd think she'd be grateful that perfect strangers were willing to pray for her recovery.

"How did you get that?"

If the plastic knife were as sharp as Janice's tone, Izzy could have cut through that rubbery chicken like butter. Her eyes darted to her mother. "How did I get what?"

"Your grandmother's necklace."

Izzy's hand moved to her neck, fingers closing around the three rings. When she got ready for church that morning, she'd proudly put the necklace on. But she forgot she'd be going straight from church to the hospital. Izzy didn't want her mother to see it before she could tell her, so somewhere between the parking lot and the hospital entrance she'd tucked it underneath the scoop neck of her sweater. It must have slipped out while she tackled the chicken.

"Gran gave it to me."

Janice's lips pressed into a thin line, the skin around them growing white.

Izzy controlled the urge to sigh. She'd messed up. She should have told her mother about the gift right away. But how would that have gone? *Hi, Mom. How are you feeling? Check out the awesome necklace that Gran probably should have left to you but she gave to me instead.* Not very tactful, but most likely wouldn't have garnered a much stronger reaction.

"Mom, I —"

The opening notes of Beethoven's Fifth sang out as Janice's cell phone vibrated on the stand beside the bed.

"Before you scold me, don't," Janice said. "I asked the nurse and made sure it was OK to have my phone on in here."

Izzy put her hands up. "I wasn't going to say anything." She picked up the phone and looked at the caller ID. "It's Vibrant Vistas."

Janice groaned. "I don't have the strength to deal with them right now." Without lifting her head from the pillow, she rolled it to the side to look at Izzy. "Would you talk to them?"

"Sure." She'd do just about anything if it meant they could avoid talking about Gran's latest gift. Izzy jabbed the button on the phone and held it against her ear. "Hello?"

"Janice Fontaine?" The voice on the other end was strained.

"No, this is her daughter, Isabella."

"Oh, Izzy!" Like flipping a light switch, the woman's tone became bright and upbeat. "It's Laura, from Vibrant Vistas."

"Hi, Laura." After frequent visits to see Gran, Izzy was on a first-name basis with most of the folk who worked there. "My mom isn't available right now. Is there something I can help you with?"

"Well, yes. I hate to bring this up, but . . . we need to clear out your grandmother's room."

Izzy looked at her mother, who had suddenly become fascinated by the tiny pieces of meat on her lunch tray. "I thought that was taken care of."

"Not yet." Laura paused, then pushed forward, speaking so fast that all her words ran together. "I'm sorry. It's probably the last thing you want to think about right now, but we need the space."

"There's no need to be sorry. I'll be there in a few hours."

With Laura happily taken care of, Izzy disconnected the call and set the phone back on the bedside stand. "Mother?"

"Hmm?" She didn't look up from her tray.

"I thought you got everything out of Gran's room."

Janice dropped her fork on the plate and fell back against the mattress, eyes closed. "I tried. But every time I thought about it, it overwhelmed me. I just couldn't bring myself to go there."

Izzy clenched her jaw, determined not to lose her cool. If Mom had just let her take care of it in the first place, like she was going to, it would already be done. But Janice had been adamant that she wanted to be the one to collect her mother's things.

"You don't understand how hard it is for me," her mother continued. "She never wanted me around when she was alive, so why would she want me going through her things now that she's gone?"

"I know you and Gran had a complicated relationship. But no matter what problems you had, she loved you. And I love you. But right now, I have to go." *And clean up the mess you left for me.* Izzy kissed her mother on the forehead and headed for the door.

"Izzy."

She turned around. Mom looked so pitiful, but the look on her face was hopeful, like she had something earth-shattering to say. "What, Mom?"

"Do you know when Brandon's going to

get here?"

Izzy's shoulders drooped. "No. But I'll call him on my way out."

"Well now, this is a surprise."

The smile on Virgil's face gave Izzy the emotional boost she'd hoped for.

"I told you I'd come visit." She held out a white bakery bag. "And I brought you something."

He opened it, looked inside, then took a good long whiff. "Ah. Fresh brownies. How did you know?"

Izzy shrugged. "I guessed. Gran used to tell me how hard it was to get something sweet here, so I'd bring her treats. Those were her favorite." She didn't think it was necessary to tell him that, despite witnessing him devour a Mallo Cup yesterday, she'd checked with the duty nurse first to make sure he was allowed to have sweets. No need to make him think she was part of the Big Brother syndicate.

"Bravo for getting them past enemy lines." He winked and put the bag on the table beside him. "I'll eat them after dinner, if I can wait that long." He sat back, interlocking his fingers across his stomach. "How's your mother feeling?"

"Not great. But she'll survive."

91

Virgil smiled. "And so will you."

"I don't know," she said with a chuckle. "We haven't lived under the same roof in a very long time. Once she moves in, you may hear the explosion all the way over here."

"It can't be that bad. Besides, Thanksgiving is just a few days away. That should help smooth things over."

"It'll probably just make it worse. This will be our first Thanksgiving without Gran."

"I take it she presided over the holidays."

Sadness pinged through Izzy's heart. "She did. She and my mom barely spoke the rest of the year, but on Thanksgiving, we all got together, no matter what. Gran cooked a big meal and afterward we decorated her Christmas tree." The thought of being in the house on Thanksgiving without Gran pushed all the air from her lungs. How would she do it this year? "It's all on me now. And I'm a terrible cook."

Virgil patted her hand. "You're probably better than you think. But you could always resort to having a traditional Logan family Thanksgiving celebration."

"And what's that?"

"Heading over to Denny's."

Her eyes grew wide. "You're not serious."

"As a heart attack." He nodded sharply.

"On Thanksgiving, that's exactly where you'll find Max and me, enjoying a hearty turkey dinner with all the fixin's." He winked. "And none of the cleanup afterward."

No cleanup. The idea had merit. But then she remembered her mother's tirade about the hospital chicken and decided against it. No one else deserved to be subjected to that at Thanksgiving.

A knock sounded at the door. Virgil looked over his shoulder and called out. "Come in!"

The door opened and a young nurse with a perky blond bob poked her head through. "Excuse me, Virgil. I heard Izzy was with you."

"She's right here, Laura. Come in."

"That's OK. I don't want to interrupt." She shifted her gaze to Izzy. "Whenever you're ready, come get me. I can give you a hand."

"Thanks." Izzy smiled as Laura backed out and shut the door behind her.

Virgil's eyes narrowed. "You didn't come here just to see me, did you?"

"You caught me. I have to clear out Gran's room."

He nodded slowly. "I see."

"But I really did want to talk to you. And

before I go, there's something else I want to ask you." She leaned forward, elbow to knees. "It's about the quilt."

"What do you want to know?"

"Everything."

Virgil laughed. "I don't know if I have the strength for everything. Remember, I'm not as young as you are. Why don't you tell me what you want to know first?"

Izzy leaned back, thinking. "I don't understand how Gran could have owned something like that and never showed it to me. Do you have any idea how she got it?"

"I do." Virgil nodded slowly. "It had been in her attic for years and years, only she didn't know it."

"When did she find it?"

"A few months before she moved in here."

"That was right before she added my name to the house deed."

"She didn't want to burden you with a bunch of her old things when she was gone. So she hired a man from her church to help her sort through them. She had no idea the trunk was in the attic until he brought it down."

"And that's where she found the quilt?"

"Exactly."

Izzy nibbled on the inside of her lip. All this time, she'd thought the quilt was something Gran had grown up with, and that's what made it special. So why all the secrecy? Why did she include it with the things she brought to Vibrant Vistas but never mention it to Izzy? Why did she need to have it with her?

The provenance.

"Virgil, did Gran say if she found anything else with the quilt? Letters, diaries maybe?"

He frowned and looked away, focusing on something in the corner of the room. "Now that you mention it, I think she did." His shoulders drooped and he slowly looked back at Izzy. "I'm tired. I think I'd like to take a nap."

Biting back disappointment, Izzy rose from her chair. "That's my cue to leave. Can I help you with anything first?"

"No, I'm fine." He waved her off. "Just not as energetic as I used to be."

Izzy patted him on the shoulder as she walked by. She was almost out the door when he called to her.

"Izzy?"

"Yes?" Had he remembered something important about Gran? About the quilt?

"Thanks again for the brownies."

She pursed her lips and smiled. "My pleasure. I'll see you later."

Pulling the door shut behind her, she told

herself not to be disappointed. She could always come back to see Virgil. And maybe, just maybe, Gran's room would yield some clues. Maybe even the missing documentation. Why hadn't she thought of that before?

With renewed enthusiasm, she set off down the hall, certain she was about to find what she was looking for.

9

She hadn't found a thing in Gran's room. Nothing helpful, anyway.

There were a lot of mementos, knick-knacks that meant something to her just because they meant something to Gran. But no diaries with cracked leather bindings, no bundles of old correspondence tied together with a faded satin ribbon, nothing to give her any hint about the history of the Wild Goose Chase quilt. And now, she didn't have the time to think about it.

From the living room, a bell tinkled. Bogie barked.

"Izzy!"

Bogie continued barking. A second later, the bell rang again, louder this time.

Instead of answering the way she really wanted, Izzy bit back a groan and called out as sweetly as possible, "Just a second!"

When the nurse at the hospital suggested giving her mother a bell, it had seemed like a good idea. That way Janice wouldn't have to yell whenever she needed something. Izzy hadn't realized that not only would Mom continue to yell, she would also ring the bell for any little thing. And every time the bell rang, Bogie would bark.

Mom had been in her home for a mere three hours and Izzy was already on the verge of a major blowout. How would she handle two months of this?

Forcing a smile, she went into the living room, shushing Bogie along the way. "Are you OK, Mom? What do you need?"

From her spot on the couch, Janice looked up. With her right arm in a sling and her cast-covered right leg supported by strategically placed cushions, she looked about as pathetic as Izzy had ever seen her. "Water."

"You still have almost a full glass right there." Izzy pointed to the coffee table she'd moved into a convenient position for Janice to put everything she needed: drinks and snacks, the TV remote, her magazines, and that stupid bell.

Janice eyed the glass and wrinkled her nose. "It's not cold anymore."

Izzy picked it up and looked down. "There's still ice in it."

"Not much. It's almost all melted. Because it's not cold anymore."

"OK. I'll get you fresh water. Would you like anything else?"

"Maybe some crackers. Do you have Ritz?"

"Yes. Is that all?"

"That's plenty." Janice smiled and used her good hand to pull the blanket up higher on her chest. "You know I don't want to be a bother."

"Oh, I know." She turned and walked to the kitchen, lips pursed together.

The phone rang and she snatched it from its cradle. The number on the display wasn't familiar, but right now she'd even talk to a telemarketer if it would provide a few minutes of distraction. "Hello?"

"Izzy, it's Brandon."

"Brandon?" She looked down at the display again then put the receiver back to her ear. "Where are you calling from?"

"My cell." He sounded out of breath, like he was in a hurry. "I lost my phone and had to get a new one."

She wedged the receiver between her ear and shoulder and began searching the pantry for crackers. "Why did you change your number?"

"I decided to go with a new carrier."

"But couldn't they get you your old number?"

99

"Seriously, Izzy, do we have to play twenty questions?"

He barked out the words and she froze with the box of Ritz in her hand. "Sorry. I was just curious. Since you're obviously busy, tell me why you called."

He sighed, but didn't bother apologizing. "I need a favor."

Of course he did. "What?"

"Is Mom's car still at your house?"

"It's in the driveway."

"Great. Can I borrow it for a few days?"

Izzy was tempted to ask the caller to verify his name to make sure someone other than Brandon hadn't accidentally dialed her number. Instead, she took the risk of asking more questions. "Why would you want to do that?"

"The Coop's having engine trouble, but I don't have time to take it to the shop."

"Can't you drive one of your other cars?"

More sighing came from Brandon's side of the phone. "It's not that simple. Can I borrow the car or not?"

If it was anybody else, Izzy would have asked her mother first. But she knew what the answer would be. "Of course. Does that mean you're coming over now?"

"Yeah. I'll be there in thirty minutes."

She reached into the freezer and grabbed

100

the ice-cube tray. "Great. There's a casserole in the fridge you can heat up for dinner." The silence of his reply didn't engender confidence. "You do remember you promised to stay with her for a while tonight, don't you?"

"Was that tonight? I don't know —"

"Brandon, don't you dare back out on me."

"Is that Brandon?" Janice called out from the other room.

"Yeah, Mom," Izzy called over her shoulder.

"Let me talk to him."

"Just a second." She thumped the glass in her hand on the counter, sloshing icy water over the rim. Now that she had a free hand, she held the receiver with it and pressed it against her mouth as she moved deeper into the kitchen. "Listen, Brandon. I've got a very important meeting at four o'clock, so I need you to be here in half an hour, just like you said. And I need you to stay with her for a few hours and feed her dinner. Or else."

He snorted. "Or else what?"

"Or else you don't get the keys to her car."

If not for the breathing on the other end of the line, she would have thought he had hung up. "Fine." He spat out the syllable as if it were a bitter pill dissolving on his tongue. "But I want to park the Coop in your garage."

"Fine. I'll leave the door up for you."

He hung up without saying good-bye. Izzy set down the receiver, picked up the glass of water and the plate full of crackers, and went into the living room.

"Where's the phone?" Janice asked.

Shoot. Brandon had been acting so weird that Izzy forgot Mom wanted to talk to him. "He hung up. But he's on his way over and he's going to stay with you while I go out for a bit."

Her mother was so pleased by the idea of a visit from Brandon that she even said thank you when Izzy set down the snack. After five minutes of pillow fluffing and helping her find something good to watch on television, Izzy made the excuse that she had to get ready for her meeting and headed back to her room.

Sitting on her bed, she looked down at the Wild Goose Chase quilt. The fabric appeared so fragile that she was afraid it would fall apart if she handled it too much. So it remained folded up in the box, just as it had been when Virgil gave it to her. Now, she dared to touch it.

With the tip of one finger, she traced the

triangular shapes running after one another. On the section she could see, there were four rows of triangles, but they didn't all head in the same direction. The first and third rows went one way while the second and fourth rows went the other. It was a striking effect, although she imagined seeing the whole quilt would be dizzying. So many different fabrics, too. Many of them looked as though they'd come from dresses. They were in reds, blues, and creams, with tiny flower patterns. Some of the striped patterns made her think of men's shirts. Had the fabric come from scraps left over after sewing those garments? Or were the dresses and shirts themselves cut up after they wore out? As Max had said, what a story this quilt could tell. No wonder he wanted to get his hands on it.

Maybe she should take it along to her meeting at the museum. After everything Max had done for her at Gran's funeral, the least she could do was give him visitation rights to this quilt that he wanted so badly. And he did want it badly, if their first interaction was any indication. What if he interpreted her generous gesture as meaning she was handing the quilt over? No, better to leave it safely at home until everything was straightened out.

The doorbell rang, followed by the tinkling of mother's bell and the frantic barking of a Jack Russell terrier. Brandon had arrived. And not a moment too soon.

Izzy propelled herself from the bed, eager to get to her meeting with Max. She might be walking into unknown territory, but at least she'd be getting out of the madhouse for a few hours.

"It's two minutes since the last time you checked."

Max looked up from his watch. "Hmm?"

Tara's jet-black ponytail swayed like a pendulum as she shook her head. "You've looked at your watch about ten times in the last fifteen minutes. Are you late for a date?"

One of the things that made Tara a great assistant was her attention to detail. It also made it impossible to hide anything from her. "I'm not late. I have an important meeting at four."

"Ah. Would this meeting be with a woman?"

"Yes, but it's not a date. I'm meeting with Mrs. Randolph's granddaughter."

"About the Wild Goose Chase?" Tara was all business now. She knew just how vital the quilt was to their upcoming exhibit.

"Exactly. I need to make her understand

how important it is for her to honor her grandmother's agreement."

He looked around the room that was currently closed to the public. So much of the exhibit was already in place, but it was fragmented. Pieces of history here, unrelated artifacts and bits of days gone by there. In the same way that the quilt turned scraps of fabric into something meaningful, it would bring all these bits and pieces together into one cohesive, powerful exhibit.

"It would be a shame not to have the quilt," Tara said. "But I'm sure you can make her understand."

"I hope so."

"No worries, Boss. You have a way with people. So get out of here and get ready for your meeting."

"You sure?"

Tara looked at the paper on her clipboard, running her pen down the list of action items. "We've covered just about everything. I can take care of the rest of it. Besides, you're too distracted to be much help."

She had a point there. "I'll be in my office, then."

Tara shooed him off with a wave of her hand, her attention already on something else.

As Max went down the back hall to his

office, his attention shifted as well. Rather, it finally settled fully and completely on the person who had been distracting him all day: Izzy Fontaine. That he was fixated on her and not the quilt bothered him more than he cared to admit.

"Focus," he commanded himself as he dropped into his desk chair. He jiggled the mouse, bringing his computer screen back to life. A few clicks later, he'd opened the file containing all the information he had about the Wild Goose Chase quilt.

He'd only seen the quilt twice. The first time, Mrs. Randolph had allowed him to take it out of the box and examine the precise, hand-stitched pieces of fabric. He'd held history in his hands. After that, every time he visited his grandfather he'd stop by to see Mrs. Randolph. Every story she shared had been a gift, and he'd hastily scribbled them down as soon as he got to his car, in fear of forgetting some fascinating detail. Then he'd transferred it all to his PC. When he told Mrs. Randolph his idea of creating an exhibit around the quilt and asked if she'd consider loaning it to the museum, she'd done him one better. She promised to give it to him.

Max went back over it in his mind. Had he misunderstood? Had she ever given him any indication that she had other plans for the quilt? Or had she simply not remembered making the promise?

No. Physically, Mrs. Randolph's health had been frail. But mentally, she was razor-edge sharp. She hadn't forgotten anything.

A knock sounded and his eyes automatically slid to the clock. Four on the dot. He rose from his chair, clicking the mouse at the same time to minimize the information on the screen, then strode to the door.

"Izzy." Max hesitated, unsure of how to welcome her. A handshake was customary, but it felt a little formal. For some reason, he had the crazy urge to hug her. Instead, he thrust his hand at her before he could embarrass them both.

"Max." She barely smiled as she took his hand.

"Come in. Have a seat." He took a step back to let her inside the room. "I hope you didn't have any trouble finding my office."

"I ran into your assistant up front. She gave very good directions."

He shut the door and turned back to Izzy. Rather than sit in one of the hard chairs by his desk, she'd gone to the comfortable seating arrangement in the corner and settled onto a soft upholstered chair. From the set of her mouth and the storm clouds in her eyes, he guessed she'd had enough discomfort for one day.

"Can I get you something to drink?" He asked. "Coffee? Tea?"

"No. Thanks." She cleared her throat and clasped her hands together in her lap. "I just want to get this over with."

"All right, then." As he moved to the chair beside her, he patted the side of his jacket, checking that he had indeed tucked a handkerchief into the inside pocket. So far, he'd needed one every time he'd seen Izzy. He didn't expect today to be any different.

Max was prepared to launch into a persuasive speech about why the quilt belonged in a museum, but her guarded look stopped him. More than just the quilt situation was bothering her. "Are you feeling OK?"

She squeezed her eyes closed and sighed. When she looked back at him, some of the exhaustion in her expression was gone, replaced by determination. "My mother moved in today."

"Oh." That explained a lot. "How long will she be with you?"

"A few months. My brother is staying with her while I'm here."

"Well, that's good. At least he can help share the burden."

Izzy laughed right in his face, then quickly

covered her mouth. "I'm sorry. If you knew my brother, you'd realize how funny that is. He's only there because he has an ulterior motive. I'm just not sure what it is."

Max shifted in his chair. This was not going the way he'd hoped. Right now, Izzy was worn down by people who wanted something from her. Once they started talking about the quilt, she'd add his name to that list. It didn't bode well for their negotiations.

"But I didn't come here to talk about my family drama. I came to talk about Gran's quilt." Her eyes narrowed, as if she dared him to say the wrong thing.

"Yes. The quilt." He paused. "I can show you the letter of intent from Mrs. Randolph."

He rose from his chair, but Izzy motioned for him to sit back down. "I don't need to see it."

"Yes you do."

She jumped a little in her seat, and Max immediately regretted the strength of his rebuttal. But if she wouldn't even look at the letter, what hope did he have of convincing her that Mrs. Randolph intended to donate the quilt? None. Which would leave him with no quilt and no exhibit. "If you'd just take a moment to read the letter, then you'd see —"

"I don't need to see anything." She hurried on before he could interrupt. "Because I'm giving you the quilt."

"What?" Max sank back down and leaned toward her. Perched on the edge of the chair, his mouth gaping, he thought he must surely look like the village idiot — not far removed from how he felt. "I don't understand. You're giving me the quilt?"

She smiled. "Well, I guess *giving* isn't the right word. I'm loaning you the quilt."

"Loaning?"

"Yes. For your exhibit. And when you're done with it, you can give it back to me." Her smile slipped a bit and worry lines creased her forehead. "That's OK, isn't it? I know people do that with artwork all the time, so I figured it wouldn't be any problem."

"Oh, it's fine. No problem at all." Why hadn't he thought of it before? The only reason he wanted the quilt was to share it with the public. It didn't matter what home it returned to after the exhibit. She'd just solved all their problems. He forced himself to sit back and relax. "I just wasn't expecting this meeting to be so . . . simple."

The smile came back, accompanied by a throaty chuckle. "Believe me, I've got plenty of complications in my life right now. I'm thrilled to add a dash of simplicity whenever possible. But there's still a little bit of a problem."

"What's that?"

"I have no idea where to find the documentation Gran told you about."

OK, maybe she hadn't solved *all* their problems. Without the provenance, the exhibit would still be nice, but it wouldn't be nearly as substantive.

"I'll keep looking, though."

Her falsely bright tone and attempt at encouragement made Max smile. "I appreciate that. For now, we should probably talk about the particulars of the loan."

The door to his office burst open. Both Max and Izzy swung their heads to see Tara standing in the doorway, looking a bit pale.

"I'm so sorry," she said to Max. "I forgot Miss Fontaine was here. But the FedEx man just left and, well, you got an envelope."

Max had never seen his usually unflappable assistant in such a flustered state. "Keep it on your desk for now. I'll look at it as soon as I'm done here."

"No, Sir. This can't wait." She was all the way in the room now, holding the envelope out to Max.

Izzy stood up. "I should be going anyway.

We can finish working out the details later."

Max stood too. "You don't have to leave."

"No, you can't leave," Tara said. "You're going to want to see this, too."

They both turned to stare at Tara again. "What's gotten into you?" Max asked her, snatching the envelope from her hand. He looked down at the address label and froze. "This can't be right."

Tara's head bobbed up and down in agreement. "I know. I read the label three times. I don't know what to make of it."

"Would one of you care to share what's going on?" Izzy spoke up.

The envelope shocked Max, so he had no idea how Izzy would take it. But he had to tell her. "The return address on the label," he said, his voice cool, calm, and level, "is from Isabella Randolph. It's from your grandmother."

10

Izzy took the envelope from Max. She looked at the front, flipped it over, and looked at the back. "Weird."

"Weird?" His head jutted forward, as if he was certain he had heard her wrong. "It's more than weird. It's impossible."

Max probably expected her to be as thrown by the envelope as he and Tara were. But since Gran's death, Izzy had already received two mystery packages from her. She was starting to get used to them.

"It's totally possible." She handed the envelope back to Max. "Obviously, Gran had this ready to go before she died and she gave it to someone to send for her."

"Of course," he said.

"Absolutely." Tara rushed to agree with her boss.

Izzy held back a grin. Neither one would admit it, but they'd been a bit freaked out at the idea of receiving a special delivery from beyond the grave.

"The big question is, who did she enlist as an accomplice? One person comes to mind." She looked at Max, waiting for him to come to the same conclusion.

It didn't take him long. "My grandfather?"

She shrugged. "They were together a lot. And she did give him the quilt to give to me."

"I guess it's possible. Maybe." Max rubbed the back of his neck. "But why would he bother with FedEx? Why not just hand it to me?"

"We'll have to ask him."

Tara took a step closer and tapped the envelope in Max's hand. "You're both missing the bigger questions. Why did Mrs. Randolph want Max to have this after she was gone? And what is it?"

Max looked from Tara to Izzy. "There's only one way to find out."

He grabbed the pull tab at the top of the envelope and gave it a yank, ripping the top open. In unison, the two women leaned forward, holding their breath in anticipation. Max reached in and pulled out the contents. The women exhaled.

Another envelope. But this one was smaller and cream colored. Izzy immediately recognized the stationery. It was the same kind that had been in the box with the quilt and the package she received from Pastor Quaid.

Max removed a folded sheet of paper. His eyes scanned the print, reading it to himself.

Tara poked him in shoulder. "We can't hear your thoughts, you know."

"I'm just making sure it's not confidential."

"It's from my grandmother," Izzy said. "How confidential could it be?"

Max nodded, then read the note aloud.

Dear Maximilian,

"Maximilian?" Izzy interrupted.

Max shot her a glare from the corner of his eye. "Do you really want to make fun of my name, *Izzy*?"

Tara snickered.

Izzy held up a hand in apology. "Sorry. I just hadn't considered that Max was short for something else." Certainly not *Maximilian*.

He looked back at the note and kept reading.

By now, you've probably tried to claim the quilt, and you must be wondering if I was senile. I assure you, I am perfectly in control of all my faculties. Please trust that I have a reason for everything I have done and will do.

Izzy and Max looked at each other, and

she knew they were thinking the same thing: Gran had more surprises in store.

Dear boy, you have blessed me with your presence. You understand the importance of family, which is why I know you will understand my decision to give the quilt to my grand-daughter. You and Izzy have more in common than you know. You both have mending to do. Together, I'm certain the two of you can discover the treasure of the Wild Goose Chase.

Max faltered as his voice cracked and he pinched the bridge of his nose between his thumb and forefinger. "That's it." He folded the paper and tucked it back in the envelope. "She signed it 'With love.' "

Izzy hadn't meant to get emotional. But the cryptic message rubbed against her already raw nerves. She squeezed her eyes shut, determined not to cry in front of Max again. But a moment later, she felt something being pressed into her hand. Another of Max's handkerchiefs. That stemmed the flow of tears faster than anything else could.

"Thanks." She smiled and handed it back to him. "I'm OK this time."

He tucked it back into his jacket. "You know where it is if you need it. Tara," he said to his assistant. "Would you give us some privacy, please?"

"Sure thing." She nodded and left the room.

When the door clicked shut, Max turned to Izzy. "There's something else in here."

"What?"

He reached into the deep FedEx envelope and produced a triangular piece of dark brown fabric sprinkled with yellow polka dots so tiny they resembled pin pricks. "Does this look familiar?"

She took it from him and turned it over, rubbing it between her fingers. "The pattern doesn't, no. But the shape does." She handed it back to him. "It's just like the pieces in the Wild Goose Chase."

As he stared at the triangle his jaw tightened and the furrow between his brows deepened. Izzy had an overwhelming desire to take his hands in hers and tell him everything would be all right. It was ridiculous on a number of levels, not the least of which was she didn't even know what was wrong, so she couldn't possibly promise to fix it. But she wanted to fix it. She wanted to erase the lines of worry that pulled at his face and bring a sparkle back to his eyes. Maybe, if he knew he wasn't alone, he would feel better.

"She sent a piece to me, too."

His eyebrows lifted, but not in the burden-

117

lifted way she'd hoped. "Why didn't you tell me that before?"

"I didn't think it was important. She gave my pastor a box to give me and it was in there."

"Just the quilt piece?"

"No. It was wrapped around a necklace. And there was a letter too."

"None of this makes sense." Max paced around the room as if sheer force of movement could help him solve the puzzle. "Why would she send us both pieces of fabric that look like they came from the quilt?"

"I'm certain they're not from the quilt. If they were, they'd show more wear. At the very least, there'd be stitch marks."

"That's true. But in the letter, she said we both have mending to do. What if the quilt was damaged and she wanted us to repair it?"

Izzy shook her head. "If that were the case, she could have sent the pieces to you. Why send one to each of us?"

"It seems she wanted us to work together."

If that's what Gran wanted, then she had achieved her goal. "OK, then what do we do next?"

"We need to take a look at the quilt."

"Now?" The question was unnecessary because he'd already removed his jacket from the coatrack in the corner.

"Now." He must have realized how pushy he sounded, because he took a literal step backward. "If it's OK with you, I'd like to come to your home to look at the quilt. And I'd like to see the letter Mrs. Randolph sent you."

All Izzy really wanted to do was spend a quiet night curled up in front of the fireplace with a good book. But with Mom at home, there was no chance of that happening.

"You can come over. I can't promise you my mother will be happy to have company though."

"Maybe she'll be asleep."

"I should be so lucky. Come on." She headed for the door, motioning for him to follow.

Izzy waited on the porch as Max parked his car on the street. It probably would have been better to go in first and make sure it was safe to bring him inside but she wanted to put off entering the house as long as possible.

She closed her eyes for a moment, inhaling the crisp fall air. Somewhere, a lone cricket chirped, bidding the sun goodnight and welcoming the evening. It was all so peaceful. And so temporary.

At the sound of a car door slamming, she opened her eyes. Max walked up the steep driveway, shoulders hunched and hands in his pockets. Stopping at the bottom of the porch steps, he tilted his head back, examining the house.

"This place is something else," he said. "How old is it?"

"Over a hundred years."

"I'll bet it could tell some pretty amazing stories."

"And every one of them about my family. Gran's in-laws built the house, then she and Grandpa inherited it."

Max climbed the stairs, stopping at the top to run his hand along the gray stone half-wall that enclosed the porch. "Is it yours now?"

Izzy nodded. "I'd lived here with Gran for years anyway. When she decided to move to Vibrant Vistas, she had my name put on the deed."

He raised an eyebrow. "What did your mother say about that?"

"I'll spare you the details. Let's just say it gave her one more thing to add to my list of transgressions."

Max's face softened and Izzy wished she could snatch back her words. She didn't want him feeling sorry for her. Hoping to erase that emotion, she rushed on. "After I graduated college, Gran's health started going downhill, so she invited me to move in with her."

"Not a lot of people would do that."

"It wasn't a totally selfless decision. I came to help her but it also saved me money. Turns out it was the best decision of my life. We made a lot of memories here." Her voice caught in her throat and a thousand pinpricks assaulted her nose. "So to answer your question, yes. This is a house with lots of stories. And most of them are wonderful."

Max stepped forward, his eyes reflecting nothing close to pity. "Am I going to have to offer you my handkerchief again?"

She pursed her lips and shook her head sharply, fighting against the moistness in her eyes. "I don't know why I keep doing this. I'm not a crier. But every time I'm around you, I turn into a soggy mess."

One corner of his mouth slid up into a teasing grin. "I certainly hope I don't move you to tears."

Far from it. With one knuckle, Izzy dabbed at the corners of her eyes. "It's not you. It's Gran."

Max bobbed his head, his expression serious. "Your grandmother was quite a woman.

I miss her, too, but it's good to be able to talk about her, to share her memory with someone."

"It is."

"I think she knew we'd need each other."

Max's hand rested on her shoulder and Izzy froze. The conversation had taken quite a personal turn. It was unexpected. It was a little scary. And it was intriguing.

"What do you mean?" she asked through lips that were suddenly dry.

"I keep wondering why she promised the quilt to both of us. She obviously wanted us to work together. But I think she knew you'd need someone to talk to, someone to support you."

She looked into his eyes. "Is that the answer to the question?"

"What question?"

"At the funeral, in the prayer garden. I asked why you were being so nice to me. Is that why? Because Gran wanted you to?"

His hand moved to the base of her neck, his fingers tangling into her hair. "I admit, we got off to a rocky start. But I'm finding it impossible not to be nice to you."

He leaned in closer, and for one breath-robbing moment she thought he was going to kiss her. Then the porch light flashed on, rapid-fire barks exploded from inside the house, and the front door rattled. She and Max jumped away from each other. A moment later, Brandon stepped out onto the porch.

"It's about time you got back," he said to Izzy. "I didn't expect you to bring someone with you." He addressed Max. "Have we met?"

"I'm Max —"

"From the hospital. Right." His tone made it clear he was done with Max and he turned back to Izzy. "We've got to talk. Come on."

"Brandon, you're being rude." Izzy's cheeks, already burning from her interrupted moment with Max, flamed hotter at her brother's lack of manners. "I invited Max over for a reason. Whatever you have to talk to me about can wait."

Brandon's eyes narrowed. "This wouldn't have anything to do with that valuable item you two were talking about at the hospital, would it?"

Max drew his shoulders back. "Yes, it does."

"Then I have a feeling we all want to talk about the same thing." Brandon headed into the house and called back to them. "Both of you, come in."

"I'm sorry about this," Izzy said to Max.

He ducked his head for a moment. "No need to be sorry. I can't wait to find out what's got him so worked up."

Izzy was pretty sure once they got inside and Brandon started talking, Max would wish he had waited longer.

11

Brandon might be rude and boorish, but right now Max felt like he owed him one. If not for his timely interruption, Max would have kissed Izzy.

What was wrong with him? Max had never been one to rush into things, especially where relationships were concerned. He couldn't deny his attraction to Izzy. During the short time he'd known her, she'd worked her way under his skin. But their relationship, if you could call it that, was largely professional. They hadn't even gone on a date. What made him think he had any right to kiss her?

Of course, she hadn't objected when he drew closer. If anything, she'd seemed as immersed in the moment as he was. But that could just be because of her heightened emotional state. No matter how strong she acted, he had to remember she was in a raw, fragile place. To pursue anything deeper or more personal right now would be taking advantage of her.

Blowing out a deep breath, Max followed her into the house. Brandon stood to one side; her mother lay across the couch, her right arm and leg propped up by a variety of pillows. And Izzy faced them, one fist planted on her hip while she motioned wildly with the other hand.

"What made you think you could go through my stuff while I was gone?" Her voice was unfamiliar, with a hard, angry edge. This was a side of Izzy he hadn't seen before.

Max looked in the direction she pointed, and understood. Dumped on an easy chair was the Wild Goose Chase quilt. Most of it was balled up on the seat, but the edges hung over the side, trailing on the floor. A spark ignited in his gut. He wanted to share a few choice words with Brandon, but he held back. This was Izzy's home, it was her fight, and she needed to take the lead.

For his part, Brandon was unfazed by his sister's anger. "I think a better question is, why are you hiding things from me and Mom?"

"I wasn't hiding anything. The quilt was in my room."

Janice shifted on the couch. "But you

never told us about it. Just like you never told me about the necklace."

Izzy's hands fells to her sides and her shoulders slumped. "Mom, I'm sorry I didn't tell you about the necklace. But I didn't keep it a secret, either." She glanced at Brandon. "Is that what this is all about? Did she tell you to snoop in my room to see what else you could find?"

Brandon sneered. "No. The snooping was all my idea."

Max didn't enjoy being an audience to their family drama. The best thing would be if he excused himself right now. But he'd come there to examine the quilt for damage, a task that was even more important now that he knew Brandon had been manhandling it.

Toenails clicked on the floor and Max caught sight of Izzy's dog headed straight for the quilt. The terrier stopped, then looked up at Max. It was like the dog dared Max to stop him.

"Why?" Izzy asked Brandon. "What were you looking for?"

The dog took another step. Max locked eyes with him.

Brandon shrugged. "You never did tell me what the valuable thing was that you talked about at the hospital. So I decided to find out for myself."

"It was a gift from Gran." Exhaustion colored Izzy's words. "That's what makes it valuable."

Brandon shook his head. "Either you're playing stupid or you're naive."

The insult got Max's attention and he took his eyes off the dog. Max opened his mouth to defend Izzy but stopped short at the sound of clattering nails on the wood. The dog had reached his destination.

"No!" It took two large steps for Max to get to the dog and scoop him off the quilt. The terrier yapped up a storm. In a second, Izzy was at his side.

"Et tu, Bogie?" She looked up at Max as she removed the squirming ball of fur from his arms. "Sorry about that."

Brandon jerked his chin toward Max. "He knows just how valuable the quilt is. Don't you?"

"Historically, it's of great importance," Max said.

"Historically, huh?" Brandon picked up something from the end table beside him. "According to these, the quilt . . ." he scanned the pages, then read from one, "holds the key to a great treasure."

Max's heart sank. He was certain Mrs. Randolph had been speaking of a meta-

128

phorical treasure, but there'd be no way to convince Brandon of that. He'd seen this kind of power struggle before when one family member wanted to donate an item to the museum over the objections of others. Even though Izzy was the owner of the quilt, her family could put up enough a fuss to keep it out of his hands for a good long time.

Still holding Bogie in one arm, Izzy snatched the letters from her brother with her free hand. "You had no right to read these. They're private from Gran to me."

"A lot of stuff went from Gran to you."

That statement explained a lot. Izzy's brother was jealous. From the scowl on her mother's face, Max was certain she shared the feeling.

"This is ridiculous." Izzy started to put the dog down but stopped and motioned to Max. "Would you please take care of the quilt?"

Brandon took a step toward Max. "Wait a minute. What does your boyfriend have to do with it?"

Color bled across Izzy's cheeks. "He's not my boyfriend. Max is the director of the California Pioneer Museum. He wants to feature the quilt in an exhibit."

Max held his breath. *Don't tell him about the loan.*

"And I'm going to let him."

Max groaned. Janice mumbled something under her breath. Brandon laughed outright. "No way. The quilt is a *family* heirloom. It doesn't go anywhere unless the family agrees."

"You have no control over this, Brandon. It's my decision to make, and I've made it."

Max admired her gumption. He also knew she wasn't going to win the fight tonight. The best thing to do now was to let everyone retreat to their own corners and cool down.

"Izzy." He kept his voice low and firm, letting her know he required her attention. "I need help to refold the quilt without damaging it."

She looked at him, lower lip clamped between her teeth. Though she struggled to control her emotions, this time there were no tears in sight. This time it looked like she was fighting to keep from hitting somebody.

"Let's take it in my room. That way, we can have some *privacy.*"

As carefully as possible, he gathered the quilt in his arms and followed her down the hall. As he laid the bundle on her bed, the absurdity of the situation hit him. In the last twenty minutes, he'd almost kissed her and now he was alone with her in her bedroom. It was a first, no doubt about it.

Not that romance was on either of their minds at the moment. If the set of her jaw and the blue electricity snapping in her eyes was any indication, she was ready to go to war. Max was glad that, for the time being, they were fighting on the same side.

"I can't believe they would do something like that." Izzy paced back and forth across the short length of her room, berating herself for what had just happened. In all actuality, she should have expected it. She'd thought if she avoided Brandon's questions at the hospital, he'd forget about the mysterious valuable object. But when Brandon smelled money, he was tenacious. In the absence of her answers, he'd decided to find his own.

"Izzy."

The warm rumble of Max's voice stopped her. In her agitation, she'd nearly forgotten he was there. He leaned against her dresser, arms crossed over his chest, brows furrowed, discomfort etched across his face.

"I'm sorry." She ground the heel of her hand into her forehead as she looked at the quilt lying on her bed. "This truly is the only room in the house we could go to and get away from them. I hope you don't think —"

"Stop." His face softened and he pushed away from the dresser. "The only thing I'm thinking is that we've still got a mystery to solve and a quilt to examine. As far as I'm concerned, we're working in your office. Nothing more."

Izzy sighed. Her office. Looking at it that way made sense. "OK. So what should we do first?"

"First we make sure the quilt isn't damaged. Some of the material is so worn and thin that it could tear from the weight if one person held it up. We need to make sure your brother didn't do that. And we need to see if any of the pieces are missing."

He took something out of his front jacket pocket and tossed it to Izzy. It was a pair of white cotton gloves. "Don't tell me your mother taught you to carry these around, too?"

Max laughed. "No. I grabbed them before we left the museum. It's better for the quilt if we don't touch it too much with our bare hands. The gloves protect it from dirt and the natural oils in our skin."

Izzy was pretty sure the quilt had been touched by bare hands for at least a hundred years before this and it hadn't destroyed the fabric. Still, Max was the expert, so she slipped on the gloves.

Carefully, they spread the quilt out on the bed, Izzy on one side and Max on the other. Max was all business, checking each section, running his glove-covered fingertips gently across the stitching. Squatting on the balls of his feet, he examined the dark blue fabric binding the edges. "Fascinating."

"What is?"

"The binding is the same fabric as the back of the quilt." He carefully pulled up a corner and draped it across the top of the quilt so both the top and the underside showed.

Izzy leaned in closer. "It looks like the back was made from one large piece of fabric."

"It was. From the looks of it, I'd guess it was a horse blanket."

"A horse blanket?"

Max nodded. "Years ago, people were much more resourceful than we are now. They found all kinds of ways to reuse and repurpose things."

What would her mother and brother think if she told them their family heirloom was half horse blanket? Would that be enough to convince them they were looking in the wrong place for a cash payout? Highly un-likely.

Izzy continued looking over the quilt. Though the triangles, which had to represent geese, chased one another in rows along the edges, they angled and turned the closer in they got. The pattern morphed into a jagged vortex coming to a halt in the middle of the quilt where two triangles met at their bases. The result was a faded red diamond marking the end of the journey. Or was it the beginning?

Max rose to his feet. "It's a minor miracle, but I don't think Brandon caused any new damage. And I don't see any place where the blocks are missing."

"Neither did I. But this is a little strange." She pushed down gently on the red diamond. "These two pieces look newer than the ones around them. And it feels a little lumpy."

"Hmm." Max folded his tall frame over the bed without putting any weight on the quilt. "It's not as strange as you'd think. Most likely, this was the first section to be worked on. As the quilt was handed down from woman to woman, the pattern emerged from the middle out. Over the course of twenty or so years, the original piece could have been showing wear before the quilt was ready for day-to-day use. It makes sense that this piece would have been replaced."

"Twenty years? It might have taken that long to make this quilt?"

"Or longer. Quilting was never a speedy undertaking."

"I can't imagine working on something for so long."

Max's eyes grew somber, his face clouding over. "Most people can't."

Although he stared at the quilt, Izzy was certain something else was on Max's mind. Whatever it was, he was far away from this little room in Monrovia.

"Max? Are you OK?"

He shook his head and forced a smile. "Me? Sure. I was just thinking we should find a safe place for the Wild Goose Chase."

"Why don't you take it with you?"

Max began folding the quilt, turning it over on itself so the colorful pattern on top was completely hidden. "I'd love to take it, but I can't. Not tonight."

"Why not? You'll take better care of it than anybody else."

"Your family's already upset. If I walk out with this quilt, they'll go crazy. You need to settle things with them before I can take it."

"I guess you're right." Izzy grabbed the

empty box from where Brandon had tossed it on the floor and handed it to Max. "Here. This is what it was in when Gran gave it to me."

He looked inside the shallow container, then turned it over. Izzy laughed. "You won't find any clues in there."

"Can't blame a guy for trying," he said with a shrug. He packed the quilt carefully in the box, then looked around the room. "Where can we put this so the treasure hunter can't get his hands on it again?"

His assessment of her brother drew a grin from Izzy. He had Brandon pegged. "In my closet. There's a lock on the door, although I have no idea why. It's been like that as long as I can remember."

She opened the door to a closet that was miniscule compared to contemporary, walk-in standards. Turning, she nearly ran smack into Max. She took a step sideways and pointed to the top shelf. "Up there would be good."

Once the box was safely stowed away, Izzy fished the key out of a dresser drawer and locked the door. "I never thought I'd lock this door. Glad I didn't throw the key away."

Max stood in the middle of the room, hands in pockets. "I should be going."

Izzy nodded.

"When can I see you again?"

She had no idea how to answer. Exactly what was he getting at?

"We still have a lot to talk about," he continued, answering her unasked question. "What the notes your grandmother sent you mean, the reason for the pieces of cloth, where the documentation might be . . ."

"We do have a lot to talk about."

"And it's probably best not to do it in your . . . office."

A blush heated Izzy's cheeks. If Gran meant to throw her and Max together, she was probably looking down from heaven right now with a grin plastered on her face.

"Good point. I'm off from school this week but I've got to take care of Mom. Can you come here? We could talk on the porch."

"I'll stop by after work tomorrow. Around six?"

"Great." Izzy opened the door to her room, motioning for him to follow. "Come on. I'll walk you through the gauntlet."

Janice and Brandon were unexpectedly silent as Max and Izzy walked through the room. Before leaving, Max stopped and addressed them.

"I'm sorry if my visit caused any friction. Have a good evening."

Janice frowned. Brandon raised his hand

in a halfhearted farewell. Izzy opened the door for Max, wishing she could follow him out and not have to face the awaiting family summit. She closed the door firmly behind him, then whirled on her brother.

"Brandon, you have a lot of explaining to do."

"Me? Mom was in on it too."

His innocent act was almost laughable. Only Izzy was too angry to laugh.

"She has an excuse. She's on painkillers. But you should be thinking straight. What made you think you could go through my things? Or that you have any right to claim what's mine?"

"I already told you. Gran left you everything, but Mom and I deserve our share. It was clear you weren't about to let us in on it, so I had to take matters into my own hands."

Izzy liked to consider herself a fairly levelheaded, rational person. Right now, she had the irrational desire to toss a glass of water in Brandon's face. Good thing there wasn't one in grabbing range. "You think you deserve your share?"

His stance transmitted righteous indignation.

"You really are something," Izzy muttered. "Have you ever stopped to wonder why

Gran gave me so many of her things?"

Janice motioned from her place on the couch. "Because you were her favorite."

Normally, Izzy would contradict her mother, denying that Gran played favorites. But after what happened today, she didn't bother with it. "No. It's because she knew me. She knew I loved the things she loved. And she knew you would only look at the monetary value of whatever she left behind."

They looked at her like she was crazy, and Izzy knew it didn't matter what she said tonight. She could ask them where they'd been for the last three years, while she was living with Gran. She could remind them that even though they all lived within twenty miles of one another, the two of them only made time to see Gran on holidays or if they needed something. But none of it would do any good. Mom and Brandon were sure they had been wronged, which, in their minds, certainly put their actions in the right.

She spoke to her brother. "Go home."

"We're not done here."

"Yes, we are. For now, we're done. We'll talk about it later." The later the better.

"Fine." Brandon leaned over and kissed his mother's forehead. "Take it easy, Mom. Don't try to do too much too soon."

Her droopy eyes opened a bit wider. "Are you leaving?"

"I have to go home."

"When will you be here tomorrow?"

Brandon looked over his shoulder at Izzy, silently imploring her to step in. Sure, now he wanted her help.

She shook her head. *You're on your own, buddy.*

He glared at Izzy, then turned back to Janice. "I don't think I can get here tomorrow, Mom. I've got a lot of stuff going on at work."

"Of course, your work comes first. But at least we'll see you Thursday."

"Thursday?"

Now, Izzy was ready to step in. "It's Thanksgiving. You will be here, won't you?"

"Of course." He paused. "But how will we do it without Gran?"

For a moment, Brandon's emotions were out in the open, and Izzy felt sorry for him. "It won't be the same. But we'll still be together as a family."

He nodded, then his eyes narrowed in suspicion. "Are you cooking?"

"Yes."

"Heaven help us." A grin lifted the corner of his mouth. Izzy couldn't agree more.

12

If one more thing went wrong, Max would need to head to the gym and knock the living daylights out of a punching bag. Tara had taken a few days off to spend Thanksgiving in Michigan with her family, leaving him to fend for himself. He hadn't expected it to be difficult, until the director of a museum in San Diego called about the early Mexican pottery Max had agreed to loan them. Not only could he not find the requisition, but it also seemed the pottery in question had disappeared, probably mislabeled and packed away in an obscure corner of the warehouse.

Then one of the aides had a question about the Moving West exhibit. Mainly, what information did Max want on the plaques for the Wild Goose Chase case. He couldn't tell her because he had no idea what was going on.

Things were far from great when he'd left

Izzy's house Monday night, but the idea of seeing her the next day had given him hope. They'd figure a way to work everything out. Only he didn't see her the next day. She'd called and said she couldn't make it but that she'd contact him as soon as she was available. Two days later, he still hadn't heard back from her.

Was she busy with her mother? Had her brother run off with the quilt? Or had she simply changed her mind and decided to keep it in the family, locked away in her closet?

Leaving the museum's back entrance, he checked his watch as he jogged to the car. He had told Gramps he'd pick him up at six. It was already six-thirty. One more thing gone wrong.

As Max steered his car through the congested streets of Pasadena, the quilt conundrum continued to plague him. If Izzy or her family blocked its use in the exhibit, what was he going to do? And if he did get the quilt, would he and Izzy be able to find the documentation about its creation? Could he have the exhibit without it?

When he pulled into the parking lot of Vibrant Vistas twenty minutes later, he was no closer to answers. Instead, he'd just given himself a headache.

The automatic front doors slid open for him and he strode to the reception desk. "Hi, Lucy."

The young nurse looked up from her seat and smiled at him. "Hi, Mr. Logan. How are you tonight?"

"Running late, I'm afraid."

"That's right. You're taking Virgil home with you, aren't you?"

He chuckled. "Can't keep any secrets from you."

She waved her hand at him. "That's all Virgil's talked about for the last two days. How he's breaking out of here and spending a few days with his grandson."

Max shook his head. Gramps pretended he was a prisoner at Vibrant Vistas, but moving there had been his idea. Despite his protests, Max knew he enjoyed being doted on by the staff. "I'm surprised he's not out here waiting for me."

"Oh, he's got a visitor. He may not realize what time it is."

"A visitor? Who?"

"Mrs. Randolph's granddaughter, Izzy." Lucy's voice dropped nearly to a whisper, as though in reverence to the departed woman.

So Izzy had time to visit his grandfather but not to call him back. Wonderful.

Max pulled his mouth up into a smile, fighting the tension in his jaw. "Great. I'll go back then. Thanks, Lucy."

"You're welcome," she called after him. "Have a happy Thanksgiving!"

Calm down, he told himself. You have no idea why she's here. But the closer he got to Virgil's room, the more irritated he became. The sound of laughter floating out the open door of his grandfather's room only made it worse.

"Max!" Virgil called out an enthusiastic greeting the moment he stepped through the doorway. "Look who came for a visit."

Izzy twisted in her chair, looking over her shoulder. "Hi, Max."

"Hi."

Confusion pushed down her brows at the sound of his clipped greeting. But Virgil plowed on as if nothing was wrong.

"Isn't this a great surprise?"

"Oh, it's a surprise all right." He stared down at Izzy. "Considering how busy your schedule is."

"Max, I'm sorry." Izzy stood up quickly, almost knocking the chair over. "I meant to call you, but you have no idea how stressful it's been at my house."

Actually, he did. The thought of what she was dealing with softened his heart.

"But that's part of why I came by today."

Virgil took a halting step forward, clearly displeased by his grandson's bad manners. "Don't be a ninny, Max."

Izzy choked back a laugh. Max shook his head. No way could he fight both of them. "I'm sorry, Izzy. I'm in a foul mood and I took it out on you. I was wrong."

"Bad day?" she asked.

He nodded in solemn agreement.

"Maybe this will cheer you up." Her lips bloomed into a full smile, her hands shooting out from her sides, as she made her announcement. "I want you to join us for Thanksgiving tomorrow!"

Who did she think she was fooling? "You don't want to face your family alone, do you?"

She dropped her hands, letting them slap against her thighs. "No. But that's not the point."

He smirked, head cocked to the side.

"OK," she admitted. "It's part of the point. But I do want you there. Both of you."

"What difference does it make?" Virgil's irritation rumbled in his throat. "She's inviting us for a home-cooked meal on Thanksgiving. What's wrong with that?"

"You haven't met her family."

"Yes I did. At the funeral."

"They were on good behavior, then."

"Really? I thought the stress of the funeral was getting to them." At this revelation, Virgil turned to Izzy. "Are they worse than that?"

She sighed. "They can be difficult, yes. But they'll behave themselves if we have company."

"Excuse me," Max raised his hand as if answering a question in class. "In case you forgot, they have a pretty low opinion of me. I doubt they'll want me to share your holiday."

"Brandon will just be happy not to be outnumbered by females. Besides, if you spend time with them, they can get to know you and realize how silly it is to fight about loaning you the quilt." She fluttered her eyelashes, then said in an exaggerated sing-song, "It'll keep you out of Denny's this year."

Max wasn't sure how eating turkey together would endear him to her brother. But any plan that kept him and Virgil out of Denny's definitely had merit.

"What time should we be there?"

Despite Izzy's positive attitude in front of Max and Virgil, there was no doubt having

146

them over for Thanksgiving would be tricky. It was a crazy idea to begin with. But something in her spirit had kept nagging her to invite them. It was as though God wanted Max and Virgil to be included in her family celebration and she couldn't do a thing about it.

Janice had been oddly amenable to the idea, probably because of the amount of prescription drugs in her system. Brandon was the one who pitched a fit about having "that man" join their family. But after she told him that Max's grandfather had been a good friend of Gran's, he began to mellow. She took it as a sign that there might be hope for her brother yet.

As she worked in the kitchen, Izzy sent up a silent prayer of thanks. So far, everything was going well. Brandon and Max were watching a football game while Virgil and her mother alternated between chatting with each other and dozing. This left Izzy free to work in the kitchen, a task that was far more complicated than she imagined. How had Gran managed to make this all look so easy? The last few years, Izzy had helped her, but following Gran's directions here and there was nothing compared to preparing the whole meal on her own.

The oven timer sounded. Izzy grabbed pot

holders with one hand and pulled down the oven door with the other. The aroma of turkey rushed out on a wave of hot air. If it tasted as good as it smelled, then mission accomplished.

Grabbing the handles carefully with the pot holders, she lifted it from the oven. The heavy roasting pan had been hard to wrangle into the oven when it was cold, but now that the hot surface allowed fewer gripping spots, Izzy found it even more difficult. To make matters worse, she hadn't stopped to think where she would put it once she had it out. There was one open burner on the stove, and she plunked the roaster down on it with clatter.

"Are you OK in there?" Max's voice called from the living room.

She called over her shoulder. "Yes. I'm fine. I . . . ouch!"

She hadn't noticed how close her hand was to the pot of simmering green beans. Yanking her hand back and holding it tightly against her chest, she sucked in a deep breath. A moment later, Max stood in the kitchen doorway.

"You don't sound fine."

Izzy shook her head. "I burned my hand a little. It's no big deal."

Max frowned and strode to the sink. He

turned on the faucet full blast and motioned her over. "Put your hand in the cold water."

"It's really no big deal." Even as she protested, she did as he said, and was glad the minute the cold water began to ease the sting.

"Let me see." With her hand still under the water flow, he took it in his, turning it over gently and examining it. "Doesn't look like you did any permanent damage."

"It feels better already."

"Good."

They stood that way, her hand in his, water pouring over both of them, until they simultaneously realized how awkward it was. Izzy pulled her hand away. Max smiled, ducking his head slightly and turning off the faucet. She ripped a length of paper towel off the roll and handed it to him.

"Thanks for coming to my rescue."

"Any time." He looked across the counters and at the stove top. "What can I do to help?"

"You don't need to do anything. Enjoy the football game."

Max leaned against the counter. "I'm not nearly as involved in it as your brother is." He looked into the living room, then said in a whisper, "Between you and me, I think he's got money on the game."

A shout followed by an expletive exploded from the other room, proving his point.

"I take it his team's not winning."

Max shook his head. "Not since halftime."

Izzy would have to talk to Brandon about that later. For now, she needed to focus on dinner, and if they planned to eat tonight, she definitely could use a little help.

"The only thing I still need to make is the gravy. If you can get the bird out of the pan and onto a platter, I can get to the drippings."

Max went right to work. While Izzy concentrated on making lump-free gravy, he removed pots and pans from the stove, pouring the contents into the serving bowls she'd set out.

"Do you usually carve the turkey at the table or should I do that now?"

Izzy smiled. "We've never been a Norman Rockwell kind of family. If you want to carve it now, that would be great."

Twenty minutes later, Izzy shook her head in surprise at the spread of food laid out on the dinner table. When she wasn't looking Max had garnished the plain platters and bowls she'd set out. Most impressive were the cranberry-dotted orange slices circling the turkey. She hadn't even known she had oranges in the kitchen.

"This is beautiful, Max. I had no idea you were so artistic."

"One of my many hidden talents." He positioned a sprig of parsley on the sweet potato casserole. "During my first year of college, I worked for a commercial photographer. He taught me a lot about food styling."

"Something smells good," Virgil called.

"It looks good too," Izzy called back. "Dinner's ready."

As Virgil made his way to the table, Izzy went to where her mom sat in a rented wheelchair. "Can I help you to the table, Mom?"

"That would be nice."

Once Janice was settled at the table, Izzy looked at the empty seat beside her. "Where's Brandon?"

Janice looked around the room, then her eyebrows lifted in remembrance. "He went outside to make a phone call."

Izzy scowled, and Max rose from his seat. "Do you want me to get him?"

"No, thanks." She motioned for him to sit. "I'll do it."

She found her brother at the end of the front porch, hunched over his cell phone. A piece of his conversation made its way to her.

"I can't right now. But you know I'm good for it."

"Brandon." She called to get his attention.

He jumped, then held up one finger and spoke into his phone. "I've got to go." He hung up and dropped it in his pocket.

"What was that about?" Izzy asked.

"Nothing. Just a buddy of mine." His expression became overly animated as he walked past her. "Where's that meal you made? I'm starving."

She grabbed his arm and pulled him to a stop. "What's going on? You've been acting weird all week."

"Of course I've been acting weird. My grandmother just died." Jaw set like granite, he jerked away from her. "Let's forget this and have a nice family meal, OK?"

Izzy sighed as he stomped through the doorway. If he wanted to pretend everything was fine, she'd go along with it. But only for today, only because she wanted to provide a nice holiday for their guests. Tomorrow, life would go on as usual, and Brandon was going to spill his secret.

Whether he liked it or not.

13

Izzy's hand was warm in Max's, and he wanted nothing more than to sit there and hold it. But the prayer couldn't go on forever, and Max really should have been focusing on what she was saying.

"Thank you, Lord, for the blessings of family, and of new friends."

Max dared to peek at her out of the corner of his eye and found she was looking right at him. Caught in the act, she smiled and squeezed his hand.

"Amen."

"Amen," the chorus of voices around the table answered her as everyone dropped hands and began reaching for bowls and plates of food.

The next ten minutes were filled with the clatter of silverware against china and murmurs of *please pass the* and *pardon my reach*. Brandon put food on his mother's plate. Then Izzy leaned over and cut the turkey into bite-size pieces for her. With something to distract them, the lingering tension between Brandon and Izzy seemed to dissipate.

Beside him, Gramps took a forkful of sweet potato casserole. "This is delicious, Izzy. So much better than Denny's."

She laughed, her blue eyes sparkling. "I'm glad you like it, Virgil. To be honest, I was worried about how it would all turn out."

"You worried for nothing," Janice said, scooping her fork into dressing and spearing turkey with her good hand. "Your grandmother would be proud."

Apparently Izzy was not used to getting compliments from her mother, because she froze, water glass halfway to her lips. She didn't say anything at first, almost like she was waiting for another comment or a *but*. When it didn't come, she smiled. "Thanks, Mom."

Max relaxed, and it wasn't until that moment that he realized how tense he'd been. He hadn't known what to expect today. But getting the chance to spend time with Izzy, learn more about her, made it worth the risk. As they sat around the table, enjoying food and making small talk, it was turning out better than he'd hoped. He even dared believe that he could come to an agreement

154

with her family about the Wild Goose Chase.

Janice dabbed the corner of her mouth with her napkin. "Izzy, did you get that box from my house?"

"I picked it up last night," she said with a nod.

"What box?" Brandon asked.

"Our special ornaments," Janice answered. "I want to put them on the tree tonight."

Virgil sat a little straighter, intrigued by the conversation. "What tree?"

Izzy swirled the last bit of her biscuit around her plate, mopping up gravy. "It was Gran's tradition to trim the Christmas tree after Thanksgiving dinner. We do it every year."

Just like that, the peace Max had settled into was yanked away. His face grew cold. He looked at Virgil but Gramps hadn't made the connection yet.

"Isn't it too early for a tree?" Virgil asked.

"It's fake." Brandon waved his hand in the direction of the garage. "I'll bring it in when we're done eating."

"Mom figured since she wouldn't have a Christmas tree of her own this year that it would be nice to put her special ornaments up here." Izzy continued talking about ornaments she and Brandon had made as chil-

155

dren, but the words faded away into a buzzing static in Max's ears until finally there was no sound at all but that of a woman crying.

Max rose to his feet, pushing his chair from the table so sharply the dishes rattled. "Excuse me."

He headed for the front door, desperate for air. Behind him, Virgil's voice broke through the fog. "Uh-oh. I should have warned you. The boy doesn't do well with Christmas."

Leaning against the porch's half-wall, Max took in deep gulps of cool night air. No, he didn't do well with Christmas. He hadn't for a very long time.

Behind him, the door opened and closed. Although his head was down and his eyes were closed, he felt Izzy standing beside him.

"This is the second time I've had to chase a man out onto this porch," she said, feigning lightheartedness. When he didn't answer, she laid her hand softly on his shoulder. "Are you OK?"

He looked at her, unsure how much to share. "I'll be fine."

"Do you want to talk about it?"

It wasn't something he normally shared. But looking into those eyes, so open and full of compassion, he couldn't hold back. "I don't have many good memories of Christmas."

Most people would prod for more details, but Izzy simply waited, giving him time to move at his own pace.

"When I was ten, my father walked out on my mother and me on Christmas Eve."

Her brows furrowed, the corners of her mouth turned down. "Max, I'm so sorry."

Stuffing his hands in his pants pockets, he straightened, pulling his shoulders back. "The worst part was what it did to my mother. She was never the same afterward."

"What do you mean?"

"She cried for days. She could barely function. Gramps finally convinced her to see someone and she was diagnosed with clinical depression."

Max examined Izzy's face, waiting for telltale signs of shock or disgust, but none presented themselves. Just the same open, accepting air. He continued.

"They put her on medication and it helped some. She had good spells. But every year around Christmastime, without fail, the dark cloud descended on her again."

So many years of crying, so many tears. Max had never known when it would start, but he wanted to be prepared. Wanted to help his mother however he could. That's when he started carrying handkerchiefs.

"One year it got so bad that she ran out of the house. She was hysterical, but she grabbed her keys and drove off." Max would never forget that night. Pacing, cursing at his father for leaving them, at his mother for turning his childhood into a soap opera of drama and melancholy. Calling Gramps, then falling asleep on the couch while the two of them waited for his mother to come home. Finally, the knock on the door the next morning, the sober policemen standing on the porch, arms straight at their sides.

Max shook his head at the memories. "I don't know if she meant to kill herself or if she just lost control. But she took a corner too fast and wrapped her car around a tree. Gramps took me in, and it's been him and me ever since."

"Max."

There was nothing a person could say when presented with such information. But hearing her say his name with such warmth and understanding touched him more than all the empty platitudes he'd received from well-meaning friends and relatives.

She put her hand on his forearm. "I can never know exactly how you feel, but I can imagine. My father died when I was eight."

Max's stomach flopped, and he kicked himself for selfishly believing he was the only one who had experienced loss. "What happened?"

"He was a police officer, doing his job. Wrong place, wrong time." She smiled, covering the quaver in her voice. "He saved a little girl and her mom. He was a hero."

There was no need for words. His hand covered hers and he lost himself in her deep blue eyes, swimming in emotions.

She gave his arm a squeeze and slowly pulled her hand away. "If you don't want to stay, I understand. But I wish you'd try to create some happy Christmas memories with us."

"I might not be very good company."

"You've seen my family at their worst," she said with a laugh. "I don't think anything you could do would be worse than that."

He hung his head. He'd done everything he could for so long to avoid thinking about his mother and those terrible years. Anything to push away the pain. But now, sharing it with Izzy, the burden didn't seem as heavy. Maybe he could do this.

"I think Virgil would enjoy it, too." Izzy leaned closer, trying to coax a smile out of him. "We'll probably all share stories about Gran."

"I definitely don't want to disappoint Gramps," he said slowly. "All right. I'll stay."

14

The tree was beautiful. Curled up in the easy chair, her morning mug of tea cupped in her hands, Izzy enjoyed the festive display and mulled over the events of the previous evening.

Max's revelation had taken her by surprise, but it explained a lot. Why he and Virgil were so close. Why family legacy and heritage meant something to him. No wonder Gran had promised him the Wild Goose Chase quilt. It represented family continuity and strength, something that had been lacking in his life.

Despite his resistance to joining in on a Christmas tradition, he'd seemed to enjoy himself. Trimming the tree had turned into a celebration in its own rite. Everybody had a story to tell about Gran. Most of them silly.

"Remember the time Gran decided we should make our own wrapping out of brown paper bags? After we bought all the stamps and markers, it would have been cheaper to buy wrapping paper."

"What about the popcorn-stringing fiasco? After an hour of trying we had a string about ten inches long. Epic popcorn failure."

"What about the time she took Bogie to have his picture taken with Santa? He grabbed that elf's hat and we ended up chasing him through the mall."

There was no shortage of tales to share. Before she knew it, Max had joined them at the tree, taking multicolored glass balls out of the packages and threading hooks through the loops, then handing them to Janice and Virgil to hang on the tree. When it came time to open Mom's special box, Janice had explained every piece to their guests.

"Brandon made this during his *Star Wars* phase."

"When was that," Izzy asked, "last week?"

Brandon playfully bumped her shoulder as their mother held up a lopsided TIE fighter made of Legos with a satin loop coming from the center. The glue that held it together had seeped from between the bricks, making it appear as though it had flown too close to the sun.

"And this one is Izzy's," Mom said, holding up the next ornament. "Our tiny dancer."

Izzy had grabbed the pipe-cleaner angel with the tulle tutu, hoping to hang it before Max noticed and asked any questions. She hadn't been fast enough.

"You're a dancer, Izzy?"

"Not anymore. But she used to be. She had so much promise." Janice's voice dropped, pulled down by disappointment.

Izzy answered Max's questioning look with a shake of her head. "It's a story for another time. How about this one, Mom?" The macaroni and yarn snowflake Izzy handed her had the desired effect, turning her mother's attention to how artistic Brandon had been as a child.

It was the low point in an otherwise lovely evening.

Izzy sighed. Bogie, who lay on the floor beside the chair, raised his head and whined. She reached down, scratching behind his ear.

"Do you think she'll ever forgive me for not living up to her dreams?"

The dog sneezed, and Izzy laughed.

"I don't think so, either."

Bogie jumped to his feet, ears pitched forward. A second later a knock sounded on the front door. Izzy glanced at the clock on the mantle. Who would drop by unannounced at eight in the morning?

The face on the other side of the peephole wasn't familiar. She opened the door, holding Bogie back with her foot. "Yes?"

The man on her porch wore a suit and dress shirt but no tie. He held a dark red file folder in his hand. "Sorry to bother you so early, ma'am. Do you know a Brandon Fontaine?"

"Brandon's my brother. Is he OK?"

"He's fine, ma'am. At least, I assume he is. I'm trying to find him, actually."

Why was this man looking for Brandon? And why here? "Have you tried his home?"

"Yes, ma'am. There's no one at his last known address. Do you have his current address by any chance?"

A chill hit Izzy, more than just the early morning breeze. Something wasn't right. "I can give him a message if you'd like."

The man's lips moved up into something resembling a smile, but his eyes remained hard. He opened the file and flipped through a few papers. "How about the Mini Cooper? Do you have any idea where he parks that?"

It took all the self-control she had not to turn and look at the closed door of her garage. What had Brandon gotten himself into? "I'm afraid I can't help you."

"Ma'am, the sooner I find your brother, the easier this will be for everybody."

For once, Izzy was glad Bogie wouldn't stop barking at her feet. She squatted down, scooped him up, and held him in front of the stranger at her door. "You're agitating my dog. I'm going to have to ask you to leave."

The man no longer bothered with the charade of a smile. He took a card out of an inner jacket pocket and handed it to her. "He needs to call me as soon as possible. Make sure you give that to him."

Izzy took the card, pushing the door shut as soon as her fingers were clear and flipping the knob on the deadbolt. She let Bogie loose on the floor with a plop, then peered out the slit between the curtain and the window frame. The man in the suit walked to the end of her driveway, got in a car, and started the engine. At the same time, she noticed a tow truck down the street. When the car drove away, the truck followed.

Fingers shaking, Izzy put the man's business card on the table and picked up the telephone. A moment later, she was leaving a message on Brandon's voice mail.

"I don't know what's going on with you,

Brother, but you need to come over here. Now. You've got some explaining to do."

"You've lost everything? What does that mean?"

Izzy stared at her brother, unable to process what he was telling her.

"Just what it sounds like. I'm broke."

Since Izzy hadn't wanted to talk in front of their mother, and Brandon refused to stand on the porch in case the suited repo man returned, they were left in the backyard, sitting in white plastic chairs coated in sunbaked dirt. Brandon had tried to dust his off before he sat, but it was useless.

"How can you be broke?" This was Brandon, the man with three cars and the upscale condo. The man who drank his Starbucks every morning while he checked his investments on his iPhone. "I don't understand."

He pushed back against his chair, raking his fingers through his dark hair. "I made a mistake."

"A mistake? How can you lose everything on one mistake?"

"It was a big mistake." He sighed, but it sounded more like the groan of a dying animal. "It was a Bernie Madoff-size mistake."

Izzy gasped. "Brandon, you didn't —"

"No, of course not." He waved her words away. "I'm not like Bernie. I'm like the guy he ripped off."

Relief was instantly followed by fear for her brother. His impulsive decisions had finally caught up with him. Then the pieces began falling into place.

"That's why you changed your phone number. So the creditors can't find you."

He nodded.

"What about last night? You had a bet on the game, didn't you?"

He nodded again.

Izzy shook her head in disbelief. "If you've lost everything, why did you waste your money gambling?"

"Do you have any idea what the odds were on that game? If my team had won, I would have made a nice chunk of change." He sighed. "It was a chance to move in the right direction and I took it."

"It was a foolish risk and you lost."

"I know. You don't have to remind me."

"What about the Coop? That's why you wanted to park it here, isn't it? You're hiding it." She leaned forward, fists on her knees. "You've made me an accomplice."

He scowled at her. "An accomplice to what? All I did was park my car here.

There's nothing illegal about that."

Izzy wasn't entirely sure if there was or there wasn't, but it felt all wrong. "You can't run from this, Brandon. If you do, it'll only get worse."

"What do you expect me to do?" He shot to his feet, hands cutting the air. "They want to take everything I have."

"Do you owe it to them?" She took his silent stare as an affirmative. "You have to make it right. Face it and deal with it."

His shoulders sagged; his head dropped. "I'll have to start over. I don't know if I can do that."

"Of course you can." Izzy stood up and put her arm around his waist. "You started from nothing once. You can do it again."

Resting his chin on her head, he squeezed her to his side. "You're a great cheerleader, Sis. I should have you around more often."

"Whenever you need it, Brother, I'm here for you. You're not alone."

"You promise?"

"Promise."

"Good. Stay with me while I tell Mom."

As they walked back inside, Izzy couldn't help but wonder, if the shine began to dim on the golden boy, would that make Izzy seem any brighter in their mother's eyes?

15

When Izzy promised to be there for her brother, having him move into her house wasn't what she had in mind. But when Brandon showed up the next morning with three suitcases and a garment bag — what he claimed to be all he had left in the world — she couldn't turn him away. And while they figured out where he would sleep and how to accommodate two guests in her small two-bedroom home, she thought of a way to use his predicament to her advantage.

"You want me to babysit Mom?"

"Not babysit." Izzy lowered her voice, hoping to work out the details without their mother hearing. "Someone needs to be here with her during the week while I'm at school. I was going to see if I could find somebody at church to hire, but since you're here, the problem is solved."

"I can't just stay here all day. I have to

work on getting my life back."

"And you will." She stuffed a pillow into a clean case and tossed it to him. "But it's not going to kill you to take some time to think things through. While you're here, you can consider all your options, work out a plan, do research on the Internet."

"And help Mom get back and forth to the bathroom." He punched the pillow and dropped it on the couch.

"Yes. But don't worry. It's not that bad." The bell sounded in the guest bedroom and Bogie ran around the corner, yapping. Izzy flinched. "Besides, it's only for three weeks. Then I'll be on Christmas break and you'll be off the hook."

"I don't know . . ."

Izzy shrugged. "Or you could stay at Mom's place. You'd have it all to yourself since she's here."

Brandon shook his head. "No, it's too far out of the way."

Since he was jobless and planning on accessing the Internet for much of his future work, Izzy didn't know what their mom's house was too far away from. "Those are your choices. Pick one."

She could see his wheels turning as he weighed his options. If he was as broke as he claimed to be, he didn't have many.

Which made it easier for him to come to a decision.

"I only have to sit with her for three weeks? Then you'll take over?"

"Yes."

"OK. I'll do it."

The bell pealed again. Bogie barked louder and began trotting in circles. Brandon looked toward the hall. "How often does this happen?"

"You mean the bell and the dog? All day." She grinned at him, then picked the pillow back up. "You get the couch at night, but during the day, this is her spot." She laid it on top of a stack of folded sheets and blankets on the chair. "It's not five star, but at least it's free."

The bell rang again, accompanied by their mother yelling something about her bladder being close to exploding. Brandon cringed. "Nothing's free in this world, little sister. I can see I'm going to earn my keep."

She headed down the hall, smiling to herself. He had no idea.

Izzy expected her first day back at work to be rocky, but it went better than expected. Brandon surprised her by having coffee ready in the morning before she left. Her students welcomed her back from vacation with an array of preliminary sketches for their self-portraits. And she was able to go straight from work to the Y in order to sneak in some water aerobics before heading home and taking on the evening shift with Mom.

Moving her arms slowly through the warm water of the indoor pool, Izzy closed her eyes and concentrated on the biggest loose end in her life: the Wild Goose Chase quilt. Mom and Brandon had gotten along fine with Max and Virgil on Thanksgiving Day. Was it too much to hope that they'd have a change of heart and let her loan the quilt to the museum without a fuss?

She blew out a deep breath and began doing partial squats in the water, just enough to work her knee joints. Yes, it was too much to hope for. Especially now that Brandon's bank accounts were zeroed out and he was starting back at square one. He hadn't mentioned the quilt since he moved in, but that was only because he'd been pre-occupied. The minute she dared bring it up, his make-a-buck radar would switch on again. For now, the quilt needed to stay safely locked away in her closet.

But what about the documentation Max was looking for? Even if she were able to get around her family and actually loan the quilt to Max, he still needed the diaries

Gran had told him about. Where would she have hidden them?

Moving side to side in the pool, feeling the gentle resistance of the water, Izzy went over all the places Gran could possibly have stashed important books or papers. They hadn't been in her room at Vibrant Vistas, which left only the house. There weren't many options there. If Izzy just started looking, examining every possible location, she would have to stumble across them eventually. Unless Gran had given them to someone else to hold for her. But it made much more sense that she'd left them somewhere Izzy — and by extension, Max — could get to.

After a few more stretches, she moved to the side of the pool and climbed out on the stairs. Placing her feet gingerly so as not to slip on the wet tile, she walked to the benches against the wall and grabbed her towel. Drying off her arms and legs, she thought about Max. Maybe she should give him a call. Maybe he'd have some idea where she should start looking.

Across the room, the door from the men's locker room opened. Two men walked through. One, in shorts and a logoed polo shirt, was obviously a YMCA employee. The other wore a trench coat over his suit. Izzy couldn't understand what they were talking about, but the second she heard the suited man's voice, she recognized it.

Shocked that the person she'd just been thinking about had appeared in the pool area, his name left her lips before she could stop it. "Max?"

He turned around and looked in her direction. She raised her hand in a wave, and his eyebrows lifted. "Izzy?"

As soon as his eyes landed on her, she wondered what had possessed her to get his attention while she was wearing a swimsuit. Even though the one-piece was modest by anybody's standards, she wrapped her towel tightly around her as he moved in her direction.

"I didn't expect to see you here," he said. "How are things going with your mother?"

"Fine. Brandon's with her now."

"Glad to hear he's pitching in."

She tried to ignore the rivulet of water that rolled from her forehead to her nose and off the tip. "He doesn't have much choice."

Max grinned. "Are you blackmailing him?"

"It's a long story. But let's just say I have leverage." Izzy gripped the towel tighter as more water ran from her hair and down her back, sending a shiver up her spine.

"Sorry, I shouldn't keep you here talking while you're dripping wet." He glanced over his shoulder at the YMCA employee, then back at Izzy. "Do you have time for a cup of coffee?"

She thought that she probably shouldn't stay away from home any longer than necessary. However, another half hour or so wouldn't kill Brandon. Coffee sounded good. Coffee with Max sounded better. "Sure. There's a Coffee Bean & Tea Leaf on the corner of Foothill and Myrtle. Is that OK?"

"Sounds good. I just have to wrap up this meeting first."

"No problem. I have to put on dry clothes first."

"That's a good idea." Max laughed and reached out as if he were going to pat her on the shoulder. But he stopped before making contact and pulled his hand back. "I'll see you there."

As she made her way down the tiled hall to the women's locker room, Izzy contemplated the bizarreness of running into Max Logan at the YMCA swimming pool. It seemed destiny was determined to throw the two of them together. And this time, Gran had nothing to do with it.

16

Max glanced at the time display on the car radio as he pulled into the parking lot of the Coffee Bean & Tea Leaf. The meeting at the Y had taken a little longer than he had planned. He just hoped Izzy was still waiting for him.

The place was crowded but he saw her sitting at a small table against the back wall with her coffee in front of her. He raised a finger in greeting. She smiled and motioned for him to get his coffee. As he moved into the line, the warmth of familiarity spread through his chest. It was so easy with her. Even when no words were spoken, they had a connection. And he'd only known her for a little over a week.

He must be losing his mind.

Five minutes later, he draped his coat over the back of the chair and sat down across from her. "Sorry it took me so long."

"No problem. Can I ask what you were

doing at the Y? Thinking of joining?"

If it meant getting to see her in a bathing suit more often, he'd join in a heartbeat. "No. We're working out the details for some summer camp programs at the museum. Field-trip-type things."

"Really?" She sat up a little taller, eyes sparkling. "I lead an art camp there during the summer."

"No kidding? Is that what you teach? Art?"

She nodded. "At First Christian High. The kids keep me on my toes."

"Is that why you needed a workout after school? Blowing off some steam?"

"Not exactly." She looked down at her cup, running her finger around the rim of the white plastic lid. "I need the exercise for health reasons."

Max wanted to know more but wasn't sure he should ask. Was it too personal? Too much too soon? But her mother's words came back to him and he couldn't help himself. "Does it have anything to do with your dancing?"

He recognized a flash of pain when her eyes met his, but then it was gone. She raised her cup, took a drink. "Yes. I was diagnosed with rheumatoid arthritis when I was eighteen. That pretty much killed my dancing career." One corner of her mouth crooked up. "Mom's never forgiven me for it."

Had he heard correctly? "She can't be upset with you for being sick."

"Sure she can. She had big plans for me."

At that moment, Max wanted to drive right over to Izzy's house and shake some sense into her mother. Instead, he cradled his coffee cup in his hands, leaning closer to the table. "What about your plans?"

"Oh, I had big plans for me, too." She laughed, the way someone does when they've told a story so many times that the sad parts aren't really sad anymore. Just facts of life. "*Swan Lake, Sleeping Beauty . . .* I was going to move to New York and dance all the big roles. But God had other plans."

He frowned, working out in his mind why God would inflict a disease on a beautiful young woman just to keep her from dancing.

Izzy caught his look and moved on quickly. "Don't get me wrong. I don't think God gave me RA. But I believe he's used it."

"How?"

"I was a good dancer. I worked hard. If I hadn't gotten RA, I probably would have made it to New York. Which means I wouldn't have been here when Gran needed me. I wouldn't have had the opportunity to live with her, learn from her. I wouldn't trade the time I had with her for anything."

"Not even for Giselle?" he teased.

"Nope." She swung her head slowly from side to side.

"Not even for Juliet?"

"Definitely not Juliet. Too tragic."

He shrugged. "Sometimes love is tragic."

"Not always. Sometimes two people are meant to be together and nothing can keep them apart. Then you get the happily-ever-after ending."

For a moment, all the noise and chatter of the busy coffee shop fell away. For a moment, it was just Max, Izzy, and the strange circumstances that had brought them together. Was this meant to be? Or was it destined to be a tragedy?

"Max?"

Her voice broke in on his reverie. "What?"

"I said I've been thinking about the documentation for the quilt."

Oh yes, the quilt, the thing that should be first and foremost in his mind. "Great. Have you figured out where it is?"

"Not exactly, but there aren't too many places Gran could have left it. I didn't find it when I cleaned out her room at Vibrant Vistas." She tipped her head to the side.

"I'm almost certain it's somewhere in the house."

Max leaned back and scratched his jaw. "I'm surprised it wasn't at the assisted living facility. I assumed she kept the quilt and the documentation together."

"According to Virgil, she didn't know about the quilt until recently. It was in an old trunk in the attic. I guess they were never together."

"Or maybe they were. Have you looked in the trunk?"

"No." She frowned, creating adorable wrinkles at the bridge of her nose. "Come to think of it, I haven't seen the trunk around the house, either. I wonder what she did with it."

"Maybe it's back up in the attic."

Her eyes grew wide and he could tell they'd both hit on the same thought. "It would be a perfect spot to hide something," she said. "No one ever goes up into the attic."

"Until today." Max drained his coffee cup and grinned. "Are you up for some treasure hunting?"

As soon as they walked through the door, Brandon was ready to run, just as Izzy expected he would be. He didn't even bother asking why Max was there. He grabbed his jacket, said he was going to walk into Old Town, and out he went.

"How was your day, Mom?"

"Boring." Janice shifted in her spot on the couch.

Izzy hung her jacket on the coatrack by the door. "I thought you'd enjoy spending time with Brandon."

She frowned. "Your brother is preoccupied with money issues. He spent the whole day on your computer."

"Can I get you anything? Are you hungry?"

"No. I can wait until dinner."

Izzy looked at the time display on the front of the DVD player. She and Max had about an hour to poke around.

Janice made a show of looking around Izzy. "Hello, Max."

Max stepped forward, hand up in greeting. "Hello, Mrs. Fontaine. Good to see you again."

She nodded, then turned her attention back to the sitcom playing on the TV.

"Mom, Max and I have something to take care of, but if you need anything," she wiggled her finger at the bell sitting innocently on the coffee table, "you know how to get my attention."

"You're not taking him into your bedroom again, are you?"

A blush warmed Izzy's cheeks and Max started coughing. "Of course not. He's going to help me look for something in the attic."

She picked up the remote and pressed the mute button. "What are you looking for? Or is this another secret?"

If she could, Izzy would keep the whole thing a secret. But she knew that wouldn't work. "I'd rather not say now. But if we find what we're looking for, I promise to tell you. OK?"

"I guess it has to be." She pointed the remote at the television, bringing the volume back on louder than it had been before. Izzy took that as their cue to leave.

She crooked her finger at Max. "Follow me."

The attic entrance was through a small door in the hallway ceiling. Max was able to reach it just by reaching up and stretching.

"One good thing about old houses with low ceilings," he said.

A built-in ladder extended down from the door. Izzy looked up into the dark opening. "We need some light." She opened the linen closet behind her and grabbed a flashlight from the bottom shelf.

"Do you want me to go up?" Max asked.

"I can do it. We wouldn't want you to get your fancy suit dirty."

He rolled his eyes at her joke. "Fine. Just be careful."

She handed him the flashlight. "Hold this until I get up there."

Izzy had never ventured into the attic. The ladder looked rickety, but if one of the men from church had climbed it without incident, it had to be strong enough to hold her. Putting her foot on the first rung, she grasped the sides and pulled herself up. The wood groaned and complained, but it held, so she continued. At the top she reached down and took the flashlight from Max.

Just as she put her head through the hole in the ceiling, Max called out to her. "Watch out for bats."

"Excuse me?" Izzy ducked back down, dropping the flashlight. Thankfully, Max had quick reflexes and caught it.

"Sorry," he laughed. "I couldn't resist."

She frowned as she took the flashlight back. "Smart aleck."

Once her shoulders cleared the opening, she shone the light around the mostly unfinished attic space. The slanted peaks of the roof were puffy with pink insulation and the wooden plank floor was covered in a thin layer of dust. At first, Izzy thought the room was empty, but then she saw the trunk, pushed against the far wall.

"It's here," she called down. She climbed the rest of the way in and crawled across the floor.

"Izzy. What are you doing? I . . ."

The farther she went, the more muffled Max's voice became until she no longer understood what he was saying. Sitting in front of the trunk, Izzy took a deep breath, which she instantly regretted. Her bout of coughing brought more muttering from below, then the creaking of the ladder.

Max's head popped up through the floor. "Are you OK?"

She nodded and waved the flashlight at him. "I'm fine. I found the trunk."

He shielded his eyes with one hand. "Point that thing in the other direction. I'm coming in."

He'd left his suit jacket below, but Izzy was sure his pants would be ruined after he maneuvered himself through the cramped, dirty space. Still, she was glad he'd come to join her. They should be doing this together.

When he reached her, he took the flashlight and shone it on the front of the trunk. She put her hand on the cold brass latch, then looked at him.

"Ready?"

"Ready."

She pulled up the latch and pushed on the cracked leather lid. It swung back, coming to a stop when it hit the wall. Together, they leaned forward, hanging their heads over the side. It was mostly empty — except for one small package, wrapped in brown paper and tied with a piece of twine.

A gift from Gran.

Izzy's hand shook just a bit as she removed the package from the trunk. "Do you think this is it?"

Max stared at it. "I don't know. Open it and find out."

There was no name on the package, no card to indicate who Gran had hoped would find it. But it stood to reason that since she left the house to Izzy, and the trunk was in the house, then the gift in the trunk was also meant for Izzy.

"Gran certainly was full of surprises," she muttered as she tugged on the end of the twine bow.

Beneath the brown paper was a book-shaped object wrapped in tissue paper. On top of that was a folded piece of stationery. Izzy held it up. "Look familiar?"

Max nodded. "It's the same as her other notes."

Izzy unfolded the paper. Max leaned closer, training the light directly on Gran's words.

My sweet Izzy,

I knew it was a risk hiding this in the attic, but I prayed the Lord would guide you. And here you are.

"How did she know you'd find it?" Max whispered.

"Why are you whispering?"

"I don't know." He cleared his throat, then spoke in his normal voice. "It seemed appropriate for the moment."

Izzy smiled. "This is how she knew I'd be reading it."

You are the only one in the family who would help Max in his search, so I'm sure you realize the documents he's looking for were once in the very same trunk as the Wild Goose Chase quilt.

The light jiggled on the page, and Izzy looked at Max.

"Once?" It was hard to tell in the murkiness of the attic, but she thought he'd gone pale.

"There's more." She continued reading.

The diaries chronicling the history of the quilt, as well as our family, are too valuable to keep together in one place. This is why I've left only one volume here. I have faith that

186

you will find the other two volumes and keep them safe.

"Three all together," Max said. "She never told me how many there were."

Remember what I've always told you: an object's true value does not come from monetary worth. It comes from the emotions and memories the object evokes in your heart.

Love,

Gran

Izzy and Max looked at each other, neither wanting to spoil the moment with more words. Carefully, Izzy pulled back the tissue paper to reveal an old book. Its brown leather cover was dry and cracked. The edges of the pages had once been embossed, but most of the gold had worn away. Pinching the corner of the cover gently between her fingers, Izzy opened the book. Immediately, a piece of the leather came off in her hand.

"I shouldn't be doing this. You're the museum guy. You do it."

She held it out to Max. He took it gingerly in one hand, passing the flashlight to Izzy. But she was so flustered she didn't realize what he was doing. It landed on the floor with a thud and a pop. The light when out, leaving them in darkness.

Izzy and Max both scrambled for the light.

187

Somehow they knocked heads.

"Ouch!"

"Sorry. Are you OK?"

"I can't find the flashlight."

From down below, the bell began to ring. The dog began to bark. Mom's voice, unable to be muffled by mere ceilings and floorboards, called out.

"What are you two doing up there?"

"Izzy." Max commanded. "Stop moving."

Izzy froze.

"Turn around."

She looked behind her and saw the open door in the floor.

"Now crawl to the light." Max said with a grin in his voice. "I'll be right behind you."

17

"That's it?" Janice asked. "That's what you were looking for?"

Max sat on the edge of the loveseat across from the couch, the diary balanced on his open palms. Beside him, Izzy looked from the book back to her mother. "It's part of what we were looking for."

After exiting the attic, Max and Izzy had stood in the hall and quickly discussed how much to tell Janice. They'd both decided the best thing was to be completely truthful. After all, the diary did contain family history, a history that concerned Janice as much as anybody else. But now, seeing the interest glowing in her mother's eyes, Izzy wondered if maybe they'd made the wrong decision.

"It's a diary that Mrs. Randolph left in a trunk in the attic," Max said.

"She wrote a diary?" Janice's eyes narrowed, as if concerned about what the book might contain.

Izzy shook her head. "No, it belonged to someone else in the family. Someone way back in the family tree."

"Who?"

Max shrugged. "We don't know yet. We haven't read it."

"And why are you interested in it, young man?" Janice pointed at him.

Max turned to Izzy. "Do you want to tell her?"

"No. You go ahead."

"Mrs. Fontaine, your mother told me there was documentation left behind by the women who made the Wild Goose Chase quilt. It's in these diaries."

"Diaries? There's more than one?"

"Yes, there are two others. We just don't know where they are."

Janice snorted. "I can tell you where one of them is."

Izzy leaned so far forward, she almost fell off the loveseat. "You can? How?"

"Because I have one of them."

Max stared at Janice Fontaine, tilting his head sideways as if he'd gain clarity from a different perspective. It didn't work. "You have one? How could that be?"

"My mother sent it to me the week before she died." Janice shrugged it off. "I didn't

190

know what it was. I thought it was one of those blank books, but then I saw writing on the pages and figured she had written something to me."

Izzy flexed her fingers, then knotted them together between her knees. "Didn't you read any of it?"

"No," Janice said with a shake of her head. "I didn't need to read all the ways I'd disappointed her and fallen short of her expectations."

Izzy stiffened. "Why would you think she'd write something like that?"

"It was a common theme with us." Janice played with the fringe on the edge of the afghan covering her lap. "It made sense that's what she would put in a book to me. But now that you've told me about the diaries, I'd be willing to bet that's what it is."

"We need to see that diary." Max said.

Izzy nodded. "Can I go over to your house and get it?"

"No need. It's in my purse."

Izzy's eyes swung to the knockoff Birkin bag taking up half of the coffee table. It was the same purse Mom had had at the funeral. "You've been carrying it around with you?"

"Since she died, yes. It was the last thing she gave me."

For a moment, Janice sounded frail and lost, a little girl who missed her mother so much that she carried around a remembrance. Izzy reached out her hand, offering comfort. "Mom, I —"

Janice must have thought Izzy only wanted the diary. Once again presenting a strong front, she reached over and nudged the purse, pushing it closer to Izzy. "Go ahead. Let's take a look."

Izzy opened the bag, moving things around in the deep recesses of the lined leather. A wallet, hairbrush, mints, makeup, tissue, travel umbrella, sewing kit . . . was there anything her mother didn't have in this purse? What would be the condition of the diary once she found it?

"Check the inner pocket," Janice said.

Izzy located the pocket and there it was. She pulled out a book wrapped in yellowing tissue paper. Beside her, Max blew out a relieved breath. Beneath the paper was another diary, this one not as old as the other. Without fear of destroying it, Izzy opened the front cover.

"Look at this." She held up a bright purple triangle of fabric. "It's another quilt piece."

Janice squinted at it. "Is that what it's supposed to be? I thought she meant for it to be a bookmark."

"We assume that's what it is," Max said. "She seems to have put these pieces in all of her letters and gifts."

Izzy nudged his arm. "There must be one in that diary, too."

Max carefully lifted the cover with one finger. Sure enough, there was a quilt piece on top of the first page. Izzy pulled it out and held it up for all of them to look at. Janice's eyes grew wide, and she leaned so far forward she looked like she could topple off the couch at any second.

"I recognize that fabric. It's from the jumper you wore in your first-grade school picture."

"Are you sure?" Izzy turned the piece of material over in her hand, examining the paisley swirls of red and orange on a pale pink background.

"Positive," Janice said. "I tried to get you to wear something else that day, but you pitched a fit. It was that jumper or nothing. Get your photo album if you don't believe me."

"It's not that I don't believe you." Izzy went to the bookcase, grabbed the album, and plopped back on the loveseat. "I just want to make sure."

Max looked over her shoulder as she flipped through baby pictures and family photos. There were so many with her mom, dad, Brandon, and Izzy, all four of them smiling and happy. But then the pictures changed, and only three remained. There were a lot less of those, and a lot less smiles.

"I don't see any dancing pictures," he said softly.

She kept her voice equally low when she answered. "That's a different album." A few pages later, she stopped. "Here we go. Good grief." She held the material up against the picture. "You were right, Mom. It's the same fabric."

"Your grandmother made that jumper for you. She must have saved the scraps." Janice held out her hand. "Let me see that other piece. The purple one."

Max handed it to her.

"This looks familiar, too. I think this came from an Easter dress Mom had years ago."

Izzy looked at Max. "Do you think all the fabric pieces we've found are like this?"

"It makes sense. That's how heirloom quilts were created. Women used pieces of leftover material and cut up clothes that were no longer wearable. Perhaps Mrs. Randolph wanted to make that connection."

"It still doesn't make sense." Izzy closed the photo album and set it on the table. "Gran only found out about the quilt six

194

months ago. Why would she have saved scraps from a jumper she made for me over twenty years ago?"

"Don't look at me," Janice said, settling back against the armrest of the couch. "She used to save all kinds of weird things. I never pretended to understand your grandmother."

"There's one more diary somewhere," Max said. "Maybe when we find it, we'll figure out how all this ties together."

"Maybe." Janice let her head flop to the side, sending Izzy a pitiful look. "I'm hungry. Can we have dinner now?"

"Sure, Mom." Izzy stood, then looked at Max. "What do you want to do about the diaries?"

"Read them, of course. But they belong to your family. The decision is up to you."

"Take them," Janice said.

"What?" Izzy and Max spoke at the same time.

"You're the antiquities expert. Take them to your museum; do whatever you need to do. Just bring them back when you're done."

Either Mom didn't believe the diaries had any monetary value or she'd gotten to the point where she simply didn't care. Izzy wasn't going to press her luck by asking which was the case.

"Here you go." She handed Max the newer diary, along with the quilt piece. "We should keep all this together."

"I'll take good care of them. They're safe with me."

"I know they are." Izzy smiled. "Call when you know something."

"I will." He turned to Janice. "Good-bye, Mrs. Fontaine. Thank you for trusting me with your family treasures."

She waved her hand in limp response. "Enjoy decoding them, or whatever it is you do." Then she turned back to Izzy. "Do we have any of that penne pasta you made the other night? That was easy to eat with one hand."

"Coming right up." Izzy ushered Max outside, waving from the front porch as he drove away. She smiled to herself as she went into the kitchen. The mystery of the Wild Goose Chase quilt, its heritage, and what in the world Gran was up to would have to wait. Janice Fontaine was ready for dinner.

18

For the next three days, Max did little more than pore over the diaries. He spent hours in his office, turning pages with cotton-glove-covered fingers, peering through a magnifying sheet, transcribing, and making digital images of important passages. The handwriting on the pages of the older diary was faded and done in such a formal, curling script that it was difficult to decipher. Janice Fontaine's joke about decoding was truer than she realized. At times, it was only by unraveling the surrounding words that he could make out particular sentences. It made for slow, tedious work. But it was fascinating.

A knock sounded on his door, and he lifted bleary eyes to look across the room. "Come in."

Tara pushed open the door, a stack of files in the crook of her arm. She looked at the fast-food containers on the coffee table and the pillows arranged haphazardly on the couch from when he'd taken a quick nap. "When was the last time you went home?"

"Last night." He'd left the museum at midnight, then fallen into his bed, only to wake up a few hours later with a revelation about a particularly troubling passage. After a shower and a quick breakfast of coffee and a bagel, he'd been back in his office.

"Really? Then I guess you've decided to grow a beard for the winter."

He rubbed his hand across his chin. Dog-gone, he'd forgotten to shave. With what he hoped was a disarming smile, he pointed down at the diary. "This is fascinating stuff."

She walked around the desk and looked over his shoulder. "How far have you gotten?"

"Almost all the way through the first diary. Or rather, the oldest of the two. I don't believe this is the first in the series of diaries."

"Why not?"

"It's not old enough. The first entry is dated June 1, 1864. From what Mrs. Randolph told me, the quilt was started in the early 1800s. Also, there's an entry in here that mentions cutting pieces of a dress to add to the quilt, which makes it sound like it was in the process of being made."

"Wow." Tara set the files on the desk, leaning closer to the old, worn pages. "Do you think every woman who worked on the quilt also kept a diary?"

"I'm not sure. I can tell you that, so far, this particular diary was only written in by one woman. It's possible that the woman who started the quilt kept a diary, then passed it on with the partially completed quilt. That may have encouraged other woman to do the same and it became a family tradition."

"It's quite a find, boss." She patted him on the shoulder. "Just don't forget it's not the only thing on your to-do list."

Max pinched the bridge of his nose and sighed. "Have I been falling down on the job?"

"A little bit. But no one noticed except me. I covered for you."

He laughed and pushed back his chair. "I could use a break and some coffee. Why don't we head to the lunch room and you can fill me in on what I've missed."

Before leaving, she gathered a handful of fast-food trash from the table. He did the same, and listened to her as they walked down the hall. She'd located the missing Mexican pottery for the San Diego museum. A local author had called, wanting to set up a seminar about the book she'd writ-ten on the spiritual significance of ar-rowheads. And the maintenance staff had put up the Christmas decorations.

Normally, the last bit of information would have brought a zing of sadness to his chest. But today, the mention of Christmas decorations didn't take him back to those black days with his mother. It reminded him of Izzy. Of hanging ornaments on her tree, her musical laughter as she explained why as a child she believed Santa Claus lived in Palm Springs, the sparkle in her eye, and how his fingertips brushed hers when she took the ornament he handed her.

"Man, you really do need a break."

"What?" They stood in the middle of the break room, and Tara caught him daydream-ing.

"You glazed over for a second." She poured him a mug of hot coffee. "Here. You should probably drink it black."

"Thanks." Holding the cup under his nose, breathing in the aroma, he looked around the room. It was cold, sterile. Not a very festive place to hang out during breaks from work. "We need some decorations in here."

"Excuse me?" Tara put the inside of her wrist on his forehead. "Are you sick? Do you have a fever?"

Max winced and pulled back. Had he really been that much of a Scrooge over the years? "It may come as a shock to you, but I'm not anti-Christmas."

Tara kept silent, but her eyes said, *You could have fooled me.*

He set down the mug, took his wallet from his back pocket, and removed a few bills. "Here. Buy some nice stuff and decorate however you'd like."

"You don't have to tell me twice." She plucked the bills from his hand and slipped them in the pocket of her blazer. "I don't know if it's from lack of sleep or change of heart, but I like the new you."

He frowned. "What was wrong with the old me?"

"Nothing. The new you is just better." She started to leave the room, but turned around in the doorway. "I almost forgot. Dalton Reed called. He wants to talk to you."

Max's eyebrows lifted at the man's name. "Did he say what he wanted?"

"No. Just left his number and said to call. The message slip is on top of those files I left on your desk." She pursed her lips as though the words she spoke were sour. "I have a feeling he's going to try to spirit you away to New Mexico. I don't like it."

He watched Tara walk away, wondering why the director of one of the country's most prestigious historical societies wanted to speak with him. Max picked up his mug and headed back to his office, wondering if the Wild Goose Chase had anything to do with it and if he'd ever be able to pull this exhibit together.

Leave it to Grant to present the most literal representation of cubism possible.

"It's made out of Legos," the boy said proudly.

"I can see that."

It was quite ingenious. Rather than create a freestanding model, the face he'd constructed using the interlocking bricks appeared to grow out of the canvas. He'd even managed a passing resemblance of himself. No small feat.

She nodded her approval. "I'm impressed."

"Thanks, Miss Fontaine."

He'd never admit it, but his smile told her he'd actually enjoyed the project.

"You've all done an amazing job." She motioned to their work lining the walls, sweeping her arm like a game show model indicating the day's big prize.

"Picasso would be proud. Monday, we'll

start looking at the exciting world of impressionism. If you're feeling adventurous, Google Vincent van Gogh over the weekend."

Izzy glanced at the clock. There were five more minutes left in the school day, but she was feeling generous. "Gather up your work and get out of here. Enjoy your weekend." In the mad dash that ensued, she waved to two of the students. "Grant. Josie. Would you two stay behind, please? I need to talk to you."

The two teenagers who stood before her couldn't be more different. Grant hitched his thumbs in the waistband of his jeans and rocked back on his heels. Josie kept her head down, eyes studying the floor, hair hanging around her face like limp brown stage curtains before a show.

"All the work was good today," Izzy said. "But you two showed some extraordinary talent."

Grant stopped rocking. Josie looked up from beneath her lashes, though her head stayed bowed.

"There's a big regional art competition coming up in February. I'd like you both to consider entering your work."

That snapped up Josie's head. "Really?"

Izzy smiled at the girl's whispered amazement. "Really. Josie, you have a very classic, polished style. But you convey so much emotion in your work. If a picture's worth a thousand words, yours is worth two thousand."

The girl's cheeks blushed until they were bright as a red velvet Santa suit. "Thank you, Miss Fontaine."

"As for you," she motioned to Grant. "You think outside of the box. Try not to let this go to your head, but you may be a creative genius."

A grin took over his face. "Cool. What do we get if we win?"

"There are scholarships for first, second, and third place. And there are several different categories. It's worth the time to enter, believe me."

She picked up two stapled stacks of paper from her desk and handed one to each of them. "This has all the rules and the entry form. Show it to your parents and think about it over the weekend. I can help you fill them out on Monday if you like."

"Cool." Grant saluted her with one finger on his way out the door.

Josie stood for a moment, looking at the papers in her hand. "You really think my painting is good enough for a contest?"

"I wouldn't lie to you. You have talent.

Now it's time to let it shine."

A smile bloomed and she pushed one side of her hair back over her shoulder. "Have a good weekend, Miss Fontaine."

"You too."

Warmth spread through Izzy's chest as she watched the girl leave the classroom, her stride more confident than she'd seen before. This was the part of teaching she loved the most. Being able to encourage young people, to help them see their God-given gifts and talents. It's what Gran had done for her.

After securing the room for the night, Izzy pulled her purse from the bottom desk drawer. Out of habit, she took out her phone, turned the ringer back on, and saw that she had a message. Praying it wasn't from Mom or Brandon, she dialed into her voice mail. To her surprise, the message was from Max.

"Izzy. Hi. It's Max. I've found some interesting stuff in the diaries. I was wondering if you'd be free for dinner tonight. So we can talk about the quilt. And eat, of course."

He rambled a little longer, left his number, then hung up.

So Max Logan wanted to take her out to dinner. He said it was to discuss the quilt and the diaries, but Izzy wondered if there was more. Was there a date hidden under the necessities of meeting? And if there was, how did she feel about that?

The fact that her heart was beating a little faster than normal as she dialed his number provided the answer.

"Max Logan."

"Max. Hi. It's Izzy."

"Izzy. Hi." The professional, all-business tone in his voice dropped and became warm and inviting. "Thanks for calling me back."

"Of course. I'd love to have dinner with you, but I can't tonight."

She thought she heard an exhale of breath. Maybe not a sigh, but a signal of disappointment. "Maybe another night."

"It's just that I promised to work down at the Friday night street fair on Myrtle tonight." She rushed on, wanting to make sure he knew that if she could see him, she would. "My church has a craft booth, and I've got the first shift."

"Oh." His tone lifted. "Well, I could meet you there. We could grab some coffee when you're done."

"I'd like that."

"OK then. It's a date."

Izzy smiled to herself. It was a date.

19

Izzy always enjoyed the street fair in Old Town Monrovia, but she loved it when it was all done up for Christmas. As she'd told Edna, the church organist who was also working the booth, it was as if the stars fell from heaven and draped themselves across the buildings and trees.

A light breeze moved the crisp night air, flapping the edges of the canopy covering the church booth. Hands in her pockets, Izzy smiled at people who passed by, but her eyes kept sweeping the crowd, looking for one familiar face.

"Izzy."

She jumped at the hand on her arm. Turning to Edna, she smiled. "Yes?"

"Goodness, dear, you were a million miles away." She held up a set of tea towels with pink flamingos hand embroidered on them. "These are marked three dollars each. Do you think it would be all right to sell two of them for five?"

"I just love them," said a woman on the other side of the table. She motioned down to the boy and girl standing on either side of her. "But I promised these two a visit to the bounce house and I don't have quite enough cash left over."

The little girl looked up at Izzy with a shy smile. It was almost enough to make Izzy want to give the towels away for free. But the money was earmarked to provide Christmas baskets for local needy families. Still, there was no reason they couldn't give this woman a hand, too.

"Five dollars for the pair would be fine."

As Edna took the woman's money and put the towels in a bag, Izzy leaned over and covertly asked if the children were allowed to have candy. When the mother nodded, Izzy reached into a bag behind the table and pulled out two candy canes.

"Here you go." She handed one to each of the children and was rewarded with face-splitting smiles. "Merry Christmas."

"Merry Christmas!" All three of them returned the greeting, and the children waved as their mother lead them off to the end of the street where the inflatable games were set up.

"Don't you just love the excitement of

children?" Edna straightened the already neat crafts arranged on the table. "It takes so little to make them happy at that age."

Izzy thought about her students. "And in about ten years, they won't be caught dead near a bouncy house. Or holding a candy cane."

A tall person walked up to the booth and cleared his throat. "I don't know. I'd be happy with a candy cane."

"Max. You made it." In jeans, a navy blue sweater, and a black pea coat, it was the most casual she'd seen him. Izzy turned to the woman beside her. "Edna, this is Max Logan. He's the director of the California Pioneer Museum in Pasadena."

"Pleased to meet you, young man."

"And you." Max pointed to the small quilts mounted on stands behind them. "Those are beautiful. Did you make them?"

"Heavens no." Edna waved a hand at him, batting her eyelashes like a schoolgirl. "We have a quilting group at our church. They mostly make small quilts for children in foster care. These quilts are special projects to raise funds for our cause."

"Very impressive."

"Max knows a lot about quilts," Izzy chimed in. "He's helping me uncover the background of a quilt Gran gave me."

Edna's eyebrows lifted. "Oh. The Wild Goose Chase?"

Izzy was shocked. "You know about it?"

"Yes, dear. Your grandmother told me all about it one time when I went to visit her. But she swore me to secrecy." Edna put her fingers to her lips and twisted, as though securing a lock.

Had Gran told everyone about the quilt but Izzy?

Edna looked from side to side, as if checking to make sure no one would overhear what she was about to say. Then she put her hand on Izzy's shoulder and leaned her head toward Max. "Did you get the envelope?"

Max's eyebrows lifted as he made the connection. "You sent the FedEx envelope to the museum."

"Yes, I did." Edna's eyes sparkled. "Isabella told me it was very important and she gave me specific directions about how long after she passed to send it. I was honored to be included in her last wish."

Another piece of the mystery solved. Izzy snaked her arm around the woman's shoulders and gave her a squeeze. "Thank you."

Before the conversation could become any more sentimental, a young woman jogged up to the booth, stopping just short of the table. "Sorry I'm late."

"No problem." Izzy said to the girl. Jordan was a college freshman with boundless energy. Having her man the booth would no doubt attract an equally energetic crowd. It was a good thing Edna was there to balance things out.

After making sure the women were settled, Izzy grabbed her purse and came out of the booth. "I'm all done here," she said to Max.

"Great." He looked up and down the street. "Where do you want to go?"

"Have you been to the street fair before?"

He shook his head. "Never have."

She looked down at the sneakers on his feet. "Glad to see you wore your walking shoes. Let's go up the street. There's a coffee shop there where we can sit outside and enjoy the lights."

"Lead the way."

They moved up Myrtle Avenue, stopping along the way to look in different booths. More than once, Izzy saw someone she knew, either from church or from the neighborhood. She and Max would stop, she'd make introductions, there would be some small talk, and then they'd move on. Izzy was so distracted by the wonderful aroma of the kettle corn cart that she tripped on a plastic strip covering a row of wires. If not for Max grabbing her arm, she would have fallen. As they continued, his hand stayed on her arm, guiding her through the crowd.

They reached the coffee shop just as a young couple was leaving their table. Izzy quickly claimed it, plunking herself down on the wrought iron chair.

"Remind me never to get in your way," Max said with a laugh.

She looked up at him with a grin. "Sometimes you've got to be quick or you miss out. Would you mind getting the drinks while I hold down our claim?"

"Not at all."

"I'd like a hot chocolate."

"Whipped cream?"

"Of course."

He smiled. "A woman after my own heart. Be right back."

While she waited for him, Izzy watched the people as they passed by. If the number of children who looked like cats, fairy princesses, and superheroes was any indication, Jonas the face painter was working overtime tonight. Across the street, a young gal with a portable sound system sang Christmas carols with such earnest, you'd have thought she was auditioning for *American Idol*.

"What a surprise!"

Izzy jerked her head to what had been an empty chair across from her. Now it contained the body of a nervous man who was trying to smile but instead looked like he was in pain.

"Barry. Imagine running into you here."

He nodded, his head bobbing so fast she feared his glasses might fly from his face. "I got my flu shot today at the school clinic and . . . hey, I didn't see you there. Have you had your shot yet?"

"No, I meant to, but I forgot."

"You should. Germs cannot be taken lightly. Anyway, Marcy was giving me my shot and she mentioned the street fair. I thought it would be fun to get out tonight. Mingle with the people."

If anyone needed to get out more, it was Barry. "That's great. Are you enjoying yourself?"

"Absolutely." The tone of his voice wasn't nearly as convincing as his proclamation.

Izzy nodded in return. What should she do? She didn't want to be rude, but there was only one extra seat at the table, and now Barry was sitting in it. How could she get him to move before Max got back?

A brown paper coffee cup appeared on the table in front of her and a hand rested on her shoulder. "Hello." Max's voice was low and deep behind her.

Izzy looked up in his general direction. "Max, this is Barry. He and I work together."

Max extended his hand. "You're a teacher, too?"

"Yes, biology." Barry half stood when shaking Max's hand, but then he plunked back down in the seat. "Say, are you the fellow who's helping Izzy with her grandmother's estate?"

"In a manner of speaking, yes."

Izzy heard the confusion in Max's voice. He probably wondered what she'd told Barry about him, whether she considered him a business contact and nothing more. Across from her, Barry showed no signs of giving up the seat. There was nothing to do but be blunt.

"Barry, Max and I are on a date."

Perhaps because she said it gently, the truth didn't register with Barry right away. A moment later, his eyes opened a bit wider as a light bulb switched on in his brain.

"Oh. You're on a . . . and I . . . you probably want this seat."

Max gave a slight nod of his head. "I'd appreciate it, yes."

"Uh, sorry." He jumped up and for some reason dusted the seat off with his hand.

"Nice seeing you, Izzy."

Barry dashed away before she could respond. Max lowered himself into the vacant seat, shoulders rising in silent laughter. "I think I scared him."

"Poor Barry. He's had a crush on me for a few years."

"I see," Max said. "So I just dashed his hopes of being with you."

The heat in Izzy's cheeks was even more pronounced because of the bite in the air. "I hope I didn't embarrass you, telling him this was a date. I just didn't know what else to do to make him move."

Max didn't say anything, just watched her as she played nervously with her napkin. Then his hand moved across the table and covered hers, stilling her fingers. "Izzy, do you think we're on a date?"

She didn't trust herself to speak. So she simply nodded.

"Good." He squeezed her fingers before pulling away. "Because we are."

She took a gulp of her hot chocolate, thankful that the whipped cream had lowered the liquid's temperature a bit. What should she say now? She wanted to ask about the diary, but would they talk about that on a date? Surely they had more to discuss than the crazy mystery Gran had

215

designed for them to solve.

"Tell me about your work," Max said, solving the dilemma for her.

She told him about her classes; about their latest foray into cubism and the surprising talent that was cropping up.

"I love seeing what these kids come up with," she said. "Especially when I ask them to use the style of old masters in a modern context. They continue to amaze me."

"I can tell you love what you do." Max swirled his coffee cup in small circles. "How did you make the leap from dancer to teacher?"

"Ah, that was all Gran." A gust of air swooshed past, and Izzy grabbed at the napkins before they could blow away. "When I was eighteen, I was rehearsing for a local production of a new ballet. I'd been having a lot of aches and pains but never really thought about it. They're all part and parcel of a dancer's life, you know?"

Max nodded.

"So one day, we were working on a particularly difficult section of the piece. I had to make a running leap into the arms of the male principal dancer. Either I didn't jump high enough or he wasn't ready. Either way, he didn't catch me."

"Ouch," Max said with a wince.

"Yeah. I landed on my right knee, hard. Normally, a fall like that wouldn't be enough to stop a dancer from dancing. But my knee swelled up and the fluid wouldn't go away. I went to my doctor, who sent me to a specialist. After a bunch of questions and tests I found out that my aches and pains weren't from dancing; they were from rheumatoid arthritis."

"That must have been a hard diagnosis to hear."

"It was. I knew my dreams of being a prima ballerina were over. I was devastated. But Gran came in and picked up the pieces."

Max set his cup aside and leaned forward. "How so?"

"She had me move in with her for a few weeks. Took care of me while my knee healed. Most important she helped me see I needed a new dream. She convinced me to go to college and find a new passion."

"And your new passion was art."

"Art is a lot like dance. It has movement, emotion. I connected with it right away." She grinned. "Unfortunately, I have no talent for creating art."

Max shrugged. "Just as well. It's a terrible career choice. There's no money in it. Not until after you die, anyway."

Izzy laughed. "True. But I do have a talent for teaching, so studying to become an art teacher made perfect sense."

"Do you ever miss dancing?"

"Of course. But I still dance. In the house, in the backyard. I just don't do it professionally." She fiddled with the lid on her cup. "Enough about me. What about you?"

"I'm afraid I'm pretty boring." One side of his mouth quirked up as he looked at her from beneath lowered lashes. "I've always loved digging into history. Went on a class trip to the Smithsonian my junior year in high school and I decided that's where I wanted to work."

"Pasadena is a long way from Washington, D.C."

"One doesn't begin a career at the Smithsonian. You have to work your way up."

She nodded. "So this is a stepping-stone for you."

"It started out that way. But after five years, I still love what I'm doing. I don't think about Washington so much anymore."

"I see." She leaned her elbows on the table, head tilted slightly. "So you may stay around town a while."

He rested his hand on her wrist, his fingers warming her skin. "The longer I'm here, the less I want to be anywhere else."

"Izzy!" At the sound of her voice being called from across the street, they both jerked back, breaking the connection.

Max muttered under his breath. "Does everyone in town know you?"

"Sorry. A lot of my friends hang out here on Friday nights." She waved at the family crossing the street. Now that she wasn't lost in Max's company, she noticed that the vendors were beginning to break down their stands and booths. "Looks like it's time to go."

Max looked around, then stood. He picked up both their cups, threw them away, and led Izzy out of the seating area. "Where's your car?"

"I didn't drive. I always walk here, then walk back home after."

"By yourself?"

"It's a safe neighborhood," she said with a laugh. "And a short walk. Takes me about fifteen minutes. It's good exercise."

"I parked two blocks over. Can I drive you home? I still want to show you what I found in the diary."

Until then, all thoughts of the diaries and the quilt had fled her mind. Even now, her only interest in them was that they would draw out her time with Max. "Sure. That would be nice."

They walked up the street, following the tide of the departing crowd. At one point, Max put his hand on her elbow to keep them from getting separated. The further they walked, the less people there were, until finally they were almost alone. So when Max's hand slid down her arm and his fingers locked with hers, she knew it wasn't for safety's sake.

They were on a date.

Way to go, Gran, Izzy thought. *I owe you one.*

20

It was the thumping that woke her.

Izzy raised her head from her pillow, peering bleary-eyed through the pale light filtering in the window. Stretching out, her hand hit paper on the bedspread beside her. She'd fallen asleep looking at the transcripts and photos Max had given her of the oldest diary. Between her date with Max and the information from the diary, it had been quite a night and a lot to absorb. Even now, her head was filled with so many facts and questions, she felt it might explode. Which made that pounding sound even more irritating.

She stuffed her feet into bedroom slippers, tied a terry cloth robe over her pajamas, and shuffled into the living room. Brandon's bedding was gone from the couch, piled in a heap on the chair. Mom sat in her wheelchair at the dining table, an open magazine in front of her and a banana in her good hand.

"Mom, I didn't hear you ring the bell."

"That's because I didn't."

Izzy rubbed the back of her hand against her forehead. "Oh. Did Brandon help you?"

"No. I did it myself."

Izzy couldn't remember the last time she'd seen such a bright smile on her mother's face. "You got into the chair by yourself and everything? That's great, Mom."

She nodded, setting the banana down on a napkin. "I'm feeling stronger. It's good to be able to do things for myself again."

The thumping grew louder and increased in speed. Izzy looked around the room, even though she knew it was coming from outside. "Do you have any idea what that noise is?"

Janice shrugged. "When I got out here, your brother was reading something on your computer. As soon as he saw me, he ran outside. I have no idea what he's doing."

Izzy didn't like how that sounded. She went to the computer hutch in the corner. The monitor was black, but a jiggle of the mouse brought it back to life. He'd left up the last site he'd been at. It was a blog about quilts, and he'd gone to one specific article: "When a Stitch, Not an X, Marks the Spot." It was all about the theory that some quilts were made not just as heirlooms or practical household items but also as treasure maps.

Brandon had seen Gran's letter to Izzy, the one that said the quilt held the key to a great treasure. Now this.

Thump. Thump.

Oh no. He wouldn't.

With no explanation to her mother, Izzy ran out the back door, letting the screen bang shut behind her. She froze at the bottom of the steps. It was worse than she had thought.

"Brandon!"

He looked up at her from where he was digging, leaning on the shovel. All around him were holes of varying sizes and depths.

"What do you think you're doing?"

Perspiration darkened his hairline, despite the coolness of the morning air; his mouth was set in a determined line. "I'm looking for whatever Gran left behind."

Izzy squeezed her eyes tightly, holding back the harsh words she wanted to fling at her brother. Taking a deep breath, she calmed herself before going on. "You think she buried a treasure in the backyard?"

"It makes sense. The quilt holds the key to a treasure. She gave the quilt to you; she gave the house to you. So the treasure has to be somewhere on the property."

"That's crazy. How could she have buried something out here? She couldn't even open a pickle jar without help."

"I don't know. Maybe she asked someone to help her. Maybe she did it years ago."

"OK, let's pretend for a second that the idea of Gran digging a hole and burying the mythical family fortune in the backyard isn't completely crazy. Even if there's something back here, how do you think you'd find it? Are you going to dig up the whole yard?"

"If I have to." His eyes narrowed, as if challenging her. "You won't let me see the quilt, so what choice do I have?"

"What choice? Brandon, this is ridiculous." As she stalked up to him, the moisture from the ground seeped through the thin soles of her slippers. But it would take more than wet feet to stop her. "There's nothing back here."

"You don't know that."

"Yes, I do." She grabbed the shovel and yanked it from his hand. He lunged for it, but not before she tossed it aside. The spade clanked against a metal birdbath that had been knocked over and rested on its side, a hole marking the spot where it had once stood. "Why are you determined to believe you can find anything valuable out here?"

"Because I'm desperate!" He shouted as he stepped toward her, hands motioning wildly. "I've lost everything! My condo was foreclosed on. I have no money. My career is a joke. I have nothing left."

Her shoulders slumped. Poor Brandon. He'd always had the golden touch, ever since the day he came home from fifth grade and announced he was going to be an entrepreneur when he grew up. He'd done it too, making the kind of business deals Izzy couldn't begin to understand. Of course he felt out of control now.

She grabbed his arm, bringing his gestures to a halt. "Do you want to know why I'm certain Gran didn't bury a treasure out here?" She waited for an answer that didn't come, but his silence told her that at least he was ready to listen. "She told me once that things don't have any value except for what they mean to us. The memories and emotions that are evoked when you see or hold an object — that's what makes it worth something."

"I don't get your point."

"Gran didn't care about money. She cared about faith. And family." Izzy motioned behind them. "What do you see when you look at this house?"

His eyes looked past her. "A wasted opportunity. Even in a down market, it's worth a bundle."

"But Gran didn't see that. This is the house her husband grew up in, the house they lived in and called home, where they raised their own child. To Gran, this house represented every tear, every laugh, every emotion of the last fifty years."

Brandon scowled, his face wrinkling in on itself. "But that doesn't mean —"

"Yes, it does." Izzy was firm. Gran told her she could bring the family together. If that was going to happen, she had to make Brandon understand. "There's no safe buried under the birdbath. No gold bars beneath the flowerbed. There is no treasure. Not the kind you're looking for."

His face softened just a tad, just enough that Izzy knew she was getting through to him.

"The reason Gran gave me the house and the quilt is because she knew I would appreciate them for the same reasons she did. Not because of the amount of money they might be worth, but because of what they represent to our family history. Does that make sense?"

He looked away, sucking in a gasp of breath and releasing it in a ragged sigh. Then he turned back to her, eyes raw with fear and confusion. "What am I going to do, Izzy? How am I supposed to start over when I have nothing?"

"Brother, you have more than you know." She put her arm around his waist, hugging him to her side. "You have your faith. You have me. And you have Mom, although that may not always be a comfort."

He laughed, but it was the most pitiful laugh Izzy had ever heard. "She's a challenge, especially now that I've disappointed her."

"I've been living with that for years. You get used to it." As soon as she said it, Izzy realized that parental disappointment was something you never got used to. She also realized something else. "You know, since she got hurt and moved in here, she seems to have mellowed."

"Really, I didn't notice."

"That's because you've been preoccupied. But something's different with her." A breeze rustled through the trees, cutting through Izzy's robe. Her teeth chattered and she wiggled her half-frozen toes. "Let's get in the house. I'll make you breakfast."

Brandon tipped his head. "Thanks, Iz. I appreciate it."

"Don't thank me yet. I expect something in return."

"What's that?"

She glanced behind them at the carnage within the tall wooden fence. "After we're done eating, you have some holes to fill in."

Max usually avoided working on Saturdays. But today was an exception.

When he'd left Izzy the night before, one thing was perfectly clear: he wanted to pursue a relationship with her. Right now, it was too complicated to move forward. With questions about the quilt and whether her family would loan it to the museum, any further attempts he made to get closer to her could be misconstrued. The last thing he wanted was for her to think he was using her as a means to an end. No, he had to know once and for all where he stood with the quilt, and then, after the exhibit was finalized, he could ask Izzy out again — this time to someplace where she wouldn't be stopped by friends every five minutes.

Max grabbed the stack of files Tara had left on his desk. Right on top was a pink slip of paper with Dalton Reed's contact information. He held it between two fingers, snapping it back and forth in front of his face. What could the man want? He reached for the phone, then stopped. It was Saturday. Not the right time for a work phone call.

Putting the message aside, he moved to the first file. It contained plans for the Going West exhibit. There was still so much information Tara needed in order to wrap things up. If they waited any longer, it wouldn't matter what Izzy's family said. Even if the museum had the quilt, there'd be no way to get everything done in time for the fund-raising gala on December twenty-first. He thought of the file on his computer that contained all the information he'd gathered on the Wild Goose Chase so far. He'd wanted to wait until Izzy formally loaned him the quilt, but if he sent it to Tara now, she could move the process along. It would make it that much easier to complete the exhibit and would enable him to go forward with what he hoped could be a more personal relationship with Izzy.

Making an executive decision, Max quickly composed an e-mail to his assistant, attached the file, and sent it whizzing through cyberspace.

He flipped through the rest of the files, then set them aside. Nothing there that couldn't wait. His first order of business was to finish transcribing the second diary. But his eyes fell back on the pink slip of paper, and curiosity got the best of him. If he was working on a Saturday, perhaps Dalton Reed was too. It wouldn't hurt to call. At the very least he could leave a message and speak to the man on Monday.

He dialed the phone and was surprised when it picked up on the second ring and a deep voice rumbled through the line.

"Dalton Reed here."

"Mr. Reed. Hello." Max cleared his throat. Why hadn't he thought to take a drink of water before making the call? "This is Max Logan, of the —"

"Logan, great to hear from you. Hold on one second."

All the sounds became muffled, but Max was sure he heard the words *over easy* and *substitute tomatoes for the hash browns.* Good grief, the man had left his cell number, and Max was intruding on his breakfast.

"Back with you, Logan."

"Sir, I'm sorry for bothering you. I didn't realize —"

"Nonsense. Wouldn't have given you this number if I didn't want you to call. But I'm out with my family, so I'll cut to the chase. I've been hearing good things about you, Logan."

"Thank you, Sir." Max had no idea where or how the man had heard anything about

230

him, but he wasn't about to argue.

"One of my best people was just snatched up by the Smithsonian, so I have a hole to fill. The opportunists are circling, but I don't want just anybody. I could use a man like you on my team."

The implications were clear. Not only was Dalton Reed offering him a highly sought-after position; it was one that could eventually lead him to bigger things. Like the Smithsonian.

"Mr. Reed, I'm flattered you'd even consider me."

"Don't be flattered. I only pick the best people for the job. And call me Dalton."

"Thank you, Dalton."

"I plan to be at your gala on the twenty-first. Need to see you in action before we make any hard, fast decisions. You understand."

"Of course. I'll have my assistant make sure you have everything you need."

The sounds of clinking and shuffling came through the phone. "Good, good. Listen, Logan, our breakfast just came. Been a pleasure talking. Take care."

The call disconnected, leaving Max to stare at his phone until the screen went black. He'd just been offered a job he didn't know if he wanted to take, which could lead to a bigger job he wasn't sure he wanted anymore. And all of it hinged on completing an exhibit with a quilt that he didn't know if he could get.

Talk about a wild goose chase.

21

It had been nearly a week since Izzy found Brandon ripping up the backyard. And even though he'd accepted that there was no treasure hidden there, she still couldn't convince him they should let the quilt out of the family's possession.

After school, she forced herself to go to the Y to exercise, but her heart wasn't in it. As she stretched and moved through the water, her mind kept returning to the quilt, and then her eyes would stray to the door from the men's locker room, as if Max might stride through, looking wonderfully out of place in his proper suit.

It was after five o'clock when Izzy trudged into her unusually quiet home. Not only was there no welcome-home barking but the TV was off as well.

"Hey, Mom." She took off her coat, unwound her scarf, and hung them both on the coatrack. "Where's Bogie?"

"Right here." She motioned to the end of the couch.

Sure enough, there was the Jack Russell, curled up in a furry white ball, his brown snout resting across her mother's leg. "He sure has taken a liking to you."

Janice smiled. "He's a good companion."

"And where's Brandon?"

"I made him move out."

Izzy meant to drop her purse on the desk chair, but instead it thumped to the floor. "You what?"

"I made him move out."

Izzy sat down slowly on the loveseat across from her. "I don't understand."

"Don't worry, he'll still come over and stay with me while you're at school. But it's silly for him to be sleeping on your couch. I told him to take my car and stay in my apartment."

"I thought your apartment was too far from his work."

Janice blew out a sharp breath. "What work? I know he's trying to rebuild his career, but most of what he's doing right now is on the Internet. He can do that from anywhere."

She had a good point. Come to think of it, Brandon probably only insisted on staying with her so he could be close to the treasure he hoped to find, the one he now knew didn't exist.

Her mother angled her shoulders, looking closer at Izzy. "I thought you'd be glad to have one less person staying here."

"Oh, it's good he's got another place to stay. I'm just surprised you suggested it."

"He was getting a bit too clingy," Janice said. "Always hovering. Like today, I wanted to read this stuff in peace and he kept asking me about it."

"What stuff?"

Janice picked up the file folder from her lap. "The diary transcripts."

Izzy nodded. She'd been disappointed the night before when Max's assistant, not Max, had brought over the transcripts from the second diary. Tara claimed Max was swamped with work, but Izzy couldn't help wondering if he was avoiding her. Perhaps their date hadn't gone as well for him as it had for her.

"I haven't gotten a chance to read any of it," Izzy said, pointing at the folder. "Anything interesting?"

"It's all fascinating." She looked at Izzy over the top of her reading glasses. "I'm finding the women wrote a lot about the interaction with their mothers and mothers-in-law. Made me realize that some things transcend time and place."

"Like what?"

"Like this." Janice thumbed through a few pages until she found the one she wanted, then she cleared her throat and read.

Mama is still upset with me. I know she wanted me to marry Earl. He's a good man with the means to provide for a wife. But there was no love there. Robert may only be a poor farmer, but I love him. I just hope that one day, Mama will understand and forgive me.

Janice lowered the pages and took off her glasses. "That was written by Clara Simons in 1891. Two years later, she and Robert traveled from Kentucky to Oklahoma and took part in the land rush."

Izzy leaned forward. "Did they get a piece of land?"

"They did not." Janice shook her head. "So they kept going west. From what she wrote, it sounds like they lived a hard life. I don't think she and her mother ever reconciled."

"That's sad."

Janice sighed. "The women in our family always seem to disappoint their mothers."

Izzy let her head drop, her cheeks flaming. "Mom, I know I disappointed you. And I'm sorry. But it wasn't my fault I got sick."

"Of course it wasn't. What are you talking about?"

Izzy looked at her mother, whose expression was one of pure confusion. "About me. Disappointing you."

"You never disappointed me."

"Excuse me?" Izzy shook her head sharply. "You've been upset with me ever since I stopped dancing."

"No, I wasn't upset." She paused, staring at Izzy for a long moment. "I take that back. I was upset. But not because you disappointed me. I was upset because, once again, another woman in our family had to give up her dream."

"Like you did?"

"Like I did." Janice blinked rapidly. "Like your grandmother did."

Izzy held her breath, almost afraid to ask the next question. "What happened between you two, Mom? What caused the rift?"

"It's not important." Janice tried to wave away her concern.

"Yes, it is. Whatever happened between the two of you has also affected the relationship you and I have. I think it's time we talked about it."

The silence stretched and grew, until Izzy was fairly certain her mother had chosen to keep her feelings to herself. But then Janice shifted on the couch, readjusted the pillow under her arm, and began to speak.

"When I was a girl, all I wanted to do was be a dancer like my mother. But I didn't have the same sense of rhythm she had, that you have, so I had to change my dream. I was going to be an actress. And I had promise. A casting director once said I reminded her of a young Elizabeth Taylor. I could cry on cue. Do you have any idea how hard that is?"

Funny that particular skill would be such a source of pride. Izzy forced back a smile. "No, I can't say that I do. I've never tried."

"Take my word for it, it's worth gold. Anyway, I took acting lessons all through high school. There weren't as many opportunities for young actors then as there are now. There was no Disney Channel, no Nickelodeon, no YouTube videos. After graduation, I skipped college because I wanted to concentrate on my career. I got a job as a waitress to support myself and I went to every audition I could. I did community theater, just to work on my craft, maybe meet some people. And that's how I met your father."

"You met Dad at the theater? I never knew he acted." Izzy couldn't reconcile the image of her strong, rough-around-the-edges father emoting beneath the bright lights of the stage.

"He wasn't acting. He was a friend of the director, and he was building the set as a favor."

"But he was a cop. What did he know about building things?"

"He worked construction for a few years before he got into the police academy. He was good at it, of course. You father was good at everything he tried." She smiled at the thought. "We were doing a production of *The Glass Menagerie.* I had the female lead, Laura. So I was always there rehearsing, and your father was always there building something."

As she talked, her eyes took on a faraway quality, as though she were right back there, meeting the man of her dreams for the first time.

"Was it love at first sight?" Izzy asked.

"Hardly." Janice barked out a laugh so loud that Bogie raised his head to see what was wrong. "I didn't really notice him, except for the times he was hammering something while I was trying to deliver lines."

"So what happened?"

"One day, the fellow who played opposite me was sick. He said he had food poisoning, but I think he had a little too much weekend, if you know what I mean. So the director asked Walt to fill in for him. Just to read the part so I could deliver my lines."

"And that's when you noticed him."

Janice smiled, the same smile Izzy remembered from the good times when she was a child. "That's when I noticed him. And he noticed me. He asked me out the next day. A month later, he asked me to marry him. And that's when the trouble started between your grandmother and me."

"I don't understand. Didn't she like Dad?"

"Nobody could meet Walt and not like him." Janice shook her head. "It was more complicated than that. You have to remember your grandmother's history. When she met my father, she was on the verge of becoming a big name in the dance world. But she gave it up for love. You see, it wasn't that she didn't like your father. It's that she saw me do the same thing she had done. I gave up my dream for a man."

"Just because you got married didn't mean you had to give up acting."

"It did if I wanted to stay married. Your father would never have been comfortable watching me fall in love with another man on stage or on a movie screen. And I don't know that I would have been comfortable doing it." She shrugged her good shoulder. "Besides, Brandon came along a year later. No time for acting with a new baby to take care of."

Izzy rubbed her palms on her knees. "I still don't understand why Gran was upset. She and Grandpa were happy. Why wouldn't she want the same for you?"

"I'm not sure. I think it brought up memories of what she could have been. Even though I know she loved Daddy and wouldn't have changed her life, she still thought about her old dreams."

"What about you? You gave up your dream, and then . . ." Izzy couldn't finish the thought.

"Then your father died. Too young." Janice drew in a shaky breath. "I loved him so much, and to lose him when we were just getting started . . . I felt cheated — of my life with him and of the dream I gave up to be with him."

A tear rolled down her mother's cheek, but this was no staged cry. This was real emotion, being shared by a woman who had erected so many walls over the years that Izzy sometimes wondered if she felt anything inside.

"When I saw the talent in you, I latched

on to it. I was determined that my daughter would realize her dream, even if I never could."

In that moment, all the questions of the last several years were answered. "And when I couldn't dance anymore, it was like watching your dream die all over again."

More tears flowed. Izzy pulled a white handkerchief from the pocket of her hoodie and handed it to her mom.

"I've been just horrid to you, Isabella." Janice pressed the material against her eyes and dabbed at her cheeks. "And now, you're taking care of me. I don't deserve it."

"Of course you do." Izzy spoke past the lump of emotion pressing against the back of her throat. "That's what family does. We take care of one another."

"You're a good daughter."

As moisture welled in her eyes, Izzy was tempted to yank the handkerchief back. Instead she leaned over, grabbed a box of Kleenex from the side table, and pulled out a tissue. "Thanks, Mom."

They dried their eyes, blew their noses, and then looked at each other and began to laugh.

"What a sight we must be." Janice looked down at the handkerchief as if she wasn't sure how it had ended up in her hand.

"Where did you get this?"

"From Max. He always has one handy."

"Ah, Max." Janice's eyebrows rose in question. "The young museum director who's so interested in your grandmother's quilt."

Izzy nodded. "Yes."

"If you ask me, I think he's interested in more than some musty old family artifacts."

Izzy looked down at the tissue, twisting it between her fingers.

Janice chuckled. "I've seen how he looks at you. And how you look back. You can't convince me there isn't a spark between you."

"What makes you so sure?"

"Because that's the way I used to look at your father."

The room became several degrees warmer, and Izzy pulled her arms out of her hoodie. "That's silly. We've only known each other a little over a month."

"That's all it took for your father and me. If I remember correctly, your grandparents were engaged after dating for only two months. How long do you need to know you love somebody?"

How long do you need? If the acrobatics inside Izzy's stomach were any indication, not more than a month. The real question was, how long do you need to know if he loves you back?

22

One more week. Izzy only had to get through one more week and then she could collapse over Christmas vacation.

The throbbing in her head continued as she trudged from the school building to her car, head down, determined to block out the noises of traffic, shouting teenagers, and thumping music.

"Izzy, wait!"

It was all she could do to hold back an audible groan. She did not have the energy to deal with Barry today.

He sprinted up and skidded to a stop beside her. After one look at her face, he hopped back two steps. "You don't look so good."

"I don't feel so good." She attempted a weak smile.

Tentatively, as if afraid whatever she had would jump out and bite him, Barry touched her forehead with the back of his wrist. A split second after making contact, he yanked his hand away. "You may have a low-grade fever. I told you not to skip your flu shot."

She couldn't have the flu. There was no room in her life for the flu. "I'm just tired. I've been pushing myself, not eating right. I need some fluids and a nap, and then I'll be fine."

"Those things certainly won't hurt." He took another step back. "Make sure to monitor your temperature."

"I will. Thanks." She unlocked the car door, then turned back to him. "Did you want to talk to me about something?"

"Oh, uh, no. Just wanted to say good-bye."

With a smile and a wave, he headed back across the parking lot. Apparently, the possibility of a communicable disease made her much less attractive to him.

She settled herself in the driver's seat, fastened her seat belt, and was just about to turn the key in the ignition when her phone rang. The phone displayed the number for the Pioneer Museum, and Izzy's cheeks burned a degree hotter.

"Hello?"

"Izzy? Hi, this is Tara."

She slumped in her seat. Again, not Max. "Hi, Tara. What can I do for you?"

"I hate to bother you, and I don't mean to push, but . . . I was wondering if you were any closer to deciding what to do about the Wild Goose Chase quilt?"

"I'm still working that out with my family."

"I see." There was a pause before Tara continued. "It's just that we need to finalize the exhibit before the gala —"

"I know."

"— and it's this Friday. We're running out of time."

"I know." Izzy squeezed her forehead with her free hand, noting that she might very well be slightly feverish. "I understand how important this is. What I don't understand is why Max isn't asking me about it himself."

Tara didn't strike her as the kind of woman who would stammer, but that's exactly what she started doing. "Max is just, um, he's very busy right now. He's spending so much time at the museum that he's been sleeping in his office. So he, uh, he asked me to give him a hand."

"Is that so?" Whether the pressure in her head was from the flu or from the idea that Max saw her as a problem to be handed over, Izzy didn't know. But she was in no mood to put up with it. "You can tell your boss that if he wants that quilt, he's going to have to ask me for it himself — in person."

"OK. But —"

"Have a nice day, Tara. Good-bye."

Izzy dropped the phone into her purse. There, she'd put her foot down, made her feelings known. And now Tara would tell Max. And Max would have to decide just how important the quilt — and Izzy — were to him.

Izzy leaned back against the headrest and groaned. What had she done?

When Izzy walked into her home and found Brandon and her mother waiting to talk to her, she knew the subject matter couldn't be good.

"Can this wait?" She kicked her shoes off by the door and trudged into the room. "I feel lousy."

Brandon slid over, making room for her on the loveseat. "Then you'd better sit down. Because this won't make you feel any better."

She dropped next to her brother, exhaling a big whoosh of air and slumping back against the cushions. "What now?"

Janice shifted on the couch. "Brandon found something today while he was doing whatever it is he does on the Internet."

"It's work related, Mom."

"That doesn't matter now." She waved a hand at him. "Izzy, just remember that we don't really know what this means. But it does look . . . suspicious."

Izzy blinked her eyes, trying to clear her head. "What *what* means?"

Brandon angled himself toward her. "You know I've been skeptical all along about the quilt and how much money it's really worth."

This again. "Brandon, I —"

"Just hear me out. I've never really trusted Logan, so I set up Google alerts for his name, the quilt, and the museum. And today I got a hit."

Her head felt heavy. None of what he was saying made any sense. "What does that mean?"

Brandon picked up several pieces of printed paper from the coffee table. "It means I found a press release about the new exhibit at the California Pioneer Museum — the exhibit that features a rare Wild Goose Chase quilt and old diaries, which were recently *acquired* by the director."

Acquired? Izzy sat forward and reached for the printouts. Before he let her have them, Brandon shuffled through the pages and put one on top.

"Look at this. It's an article about the exhibit. Read the quotation from this Dalton Reed fellow."

Izzy skimmed the paragraphs until she fell on the spot Brandon had pointed out.

Mr. Logan's doing some impressive things at the California Pioneer Museum. His recent acquisition of this heirloom quilt and the supporting diaries is quite a coup. If the exhibit's as fabulous as I expect, it will be a major stepping-stone in his career.

Until that moment, Izzy hadn't known a person could be hot and cold at the same time. Beneath her fevered skin, her blood chilled. Had everything between her and Max been a sham? Just a way to get close to her so he could charm what he wanted out of her? If so, he was making progress. He already had possession of two of the three diaries. All he needed was the quilt, and hadn't she planned to loan it to him all along?

"Izzy." Her mother's voice cut through her fog of thought. "Don't jump to conclusions. This doesn't mean anything."

Brandon scowled, jabbing at the article. "Of course it means something. It means that quilt is worth an awful lot more than Logan has been letting on. And he's using you to get it."

From his place on the couch, Bogie's head shot up, ears perked. A second later, the doorbell rang. Izzy pushed herself up from the couch and went to the door.

Max stood on the porch, smiling. Izzy's heart jumped, and then her temper flared. How dare he look so happy to see her? How dare her emotions react to him so, her lips automatically curving up into a smile?

It took all the strength she had to display what she hoped was a grim expression. "I see Tara gave you my message."

"She did. And it made me realize that not calling you has been a big mistake. Can I come in?"

"No." She shot the syllable at him.

His eyebrows drew down, as did the corners of his mouth. "Izzy, I came to apologize. And to explain."

"Oh, really? Did you come to explain this?" She thrust the paper at him, almost hitting him in the face with it.

As he squinted to make out the text under the pale glow of the porch light, Max's face changed from confusion to surprise to irritation.

"This is wrong," he said. "I never authorized this press release."

Izzy snorted. "I guess you never talked to

Dalton Reed, either." More than anything, she wanted him to confirm that he hadn't. Then maybe she could believe this was all one big misunderstanding.

Max opened his mouth to speak, then snapped it shut. He paused, looked down at his shoes, then back at Izzy. "Yes, I did speak to Dalton, but it's not what you think."

Her stomach rolled. She couldn't stand there another second. "You want to know what I think? I think you've been playing me this whole time. I think you really do have ambitions of getting to the Smithsonian and you'll do anything you need to do to get there."

"Listen to yourself, Izzy. What you're saying makes no sense." He looked past her, into the room, and pointed at Brandon. "Did you do this? Did you make up this wild story?"

Brandon raised his hands in innocence. "All I did was gather the information. I didn't make up that article or that press release. That's all on you, friend."

Max took a step forward, but Izzy stopped him with a palm to the chest. "Don't, Max. I'm sick with the flu or something. I'm in no shape to put up with this. We're done. You're just going to have to further your career without me or my grandmother's quilt."

"But Izzy —"

"Good-bye, Max."

As she shut the door, she caught a glimpse of a man who looked like he'd just lost his best friend. She knew exactly how he felt.

Because she felt the same way.

She turned to her family. Brandon looked pleased with himself, but her mother looked concerned. Before either of them could say anything, she shut them down with a wave of her hand. "I don't want to talk about it. I'm going to bed. Mom, if you need anything, you know how to reach me."

Once in her room, behind the closed door, Izzy collapsed on the bed. Head pounding, face burning, stomach churning, she let the tears come, soaking one side of her pillow. After a good amount of crying and mental arguments with herself, she fell asleep.

Three hours later, her eyes popped open. The front door had thumped shut, and now a car engine rumbled outside. Must be Brandon leaving. She looked at the alarm clock on her bedside table. Nine o'clock. Hopefully, he'd helped Mom into her room before he left. Judging by the silence, she guessed he had.

Izzy rolled over and covered her eyes with

her arm. Had she been too hasty? Had she judged Max without knowing all the facts? If it weren't for that quilt, she wouldn't be in this mess. Of course, if it weren't for the quilt and the diaries and Gran's contrived game of hide and seek, she never would have met Max.

She got out of bed, then immediately sat back down. Too quick. As soon as her head stopped swimming, she tried it again, but more slowly this time. Once she was steady, she went to her dresser drawer, removed the key she'd hidden way in the back under a pair of hardly used thermal underwear, and unlocked the closet door.

The box was so clunky and heavy that she almost dropped it as she wrestled it from the top shelf. But she managed to get the Wild Goose Chase quilt safely to her bed. She removed the lid and looked down at the family heirloom. So much trouble over such a simple item. A quilt. Something meant to give warmth and comfort. A symbol of family. There had been plenty of sacrifices and hardships on the parts of the women who made it, but also so much love.

Izzy couldn't feel any of those things now when she looked at it.

If Gran was right, that an item was only worth the feelings and emotions it called to mind, then this quilt had a negative value. There was only one way to restore positive meaning to the Wild Goose Chase and hopefully bring peace to her family.

And if she hurried, she might have just enough time to do it.

23

He'd ruined everything.

Max leaned over his desk, elbows on the polished wood, forehead braced against his hands. One phone call to Tara had confirmed the press release was a mistake. She thought he'd sent her the file so she could get the word out about the exhibit. It was perfectly understandable. As for Dalton Reed's comment, Max could only assume the man was putting on some pressure, making his wishes known in order to make it difficult for Max to say no if a job offer came his way.

He wanted to blame Tara and Dalton for the mess he was in, but he couldn't. It was his own fault. He shouldn't have avoided Izzy over the last week. He should have told her exactly what he was feeling and found a way to keep their relationship separate from the issue of the quilt and the museum. Now, not only had he lost any hope of getting the quilt, he'd also lost something far more precious: the possibility of a future with Izzy.

How had he fallen this hard this fast? It seemed like they'd known each other forever, yet it was only last month he'd shown up at her door looking for his grandfather. In that short amount of time, she'd worked her way under his skin and into his heart.

"Max!"

"Oh fine," he muttered. "Now I'm hearing her voice."

"Max!" *Thud. Thud. Thud.* "Maximilian!"

His head snapped up. He wasn't just hearing things. He ran from his office, down the hall, and through the dark museum until he could see the front entrance. Izzy stood on the other side of the double doors, her nose and fist pressed against the glass, holding the big white quilt box against her chest.

She pounded again. "I know you're in there! I saw your car!"

Max hurried forward and unlocked the door. "Izzy. How did you know I'd be here?"

"Tara told me you've been sleeping in your office. I took a chance." She stumbled forward and shoved the box at him. "Here. This is yours."

The quilt was right there, in his reach, but all Max cared about was how red her face was. "Do you have a fever?" He touched

257

her forehead and frowned. "You're burning up. Get in here."

He dropped the box on the floor, captured her wrist, and pulled her into the museum. After quickly locking the door, he turned and caught her just as she was about to collapse.

She looked up at him with glassy eyes. "I don't feel so good."

"I know, honey. I'm going to take care of you."

He scooped her up and carried her back the way he came, through the dark exhibit rooms, down the back hall, and into his office. He gently laid her on the couch and put one of the throw pillows under her head. "Wait here."

He ran to the break room, grabbed a bottle of water, and raided the first-aid kit. When he got back to the office, she was sitting up on the couch, hands braced on either side of her knees, head hanging down. When he sat beside her, she rolled her head to the side to look at him. "Why am I in your office?"

"You came to see me, but you're sick. You shouldn't have been driving at all, you know."

He twisted the cap off the water and gave it to her. "Take a drink." She did. Then he put two capsules in her hand. "Ibuprofen, to help take down your fever."

She looked from the pills in her hand back to him. "Why are you always taking care of me?"

Because I love you, Izzy. How he wanted to tell her. But right now, with her in a fever-induced haze and looking like she might throw up at any second, probably wasn't the best time. "I'm a gentleman, remember?"

"Yes, you are. You are a very gentle man." She popped the pills in her mouth and washed them down with the water. "And I am a very confused woman."

"Why are you confused?"

"It's all because of that stupid quilt." She put her hand over her mouth. "Sorry. That *heirloom* quilt."

"I understand." In the last few hours, he'd been tempted to call it a few choice words of his own.

Izzy put the water bottle on the table and leaned back against the couch cushions. "I know Gran wanted it to bring my family together, but all it's done is cause trouble." She sighed. "That's why I brought it here tonight. I'm giving it to you."

"It's wonderful that you want to loan it to the museum, but —"

"No. I'm not loaning it to the museum. I'm giving it to you."

This was a twist he never saw coming. "You're giving it to me? Does your family know about this?"

"Not yet. But it's my decision to make. Since I got my hands on that quilt it's caused nothing but strife. Did you know that my brother dug up my backyard because he thought the quilt was a treasure map?"

Max held back a smile. He could imagine Brandon frantically shoveling away like a forgetful dog trying to locate his missing bone. "No, I didn't."

"No, you didn't. Because you haven't been around since our date."

The accusation in her voice stung. "Izzy, there was a reason for that. I didn't want you to think I was interested in you just to get the quilt. So I decided it was best to keep my distance until —"

"Until you got it." Her shoulders jerked and she rubbed her hands up and down on her arms. "It's OK, Max. You don't have to pretend anymore."

"I wasn't pretending. I'm not pretending now."

"The quilt is yours." She looked behind

her and grabbed the pillow. "I need to lie down."

She bunched the pillow under her head and drew her knees up, curling into a tight ball on the narrow couch. Her body shook as a shiver rippled through her.

"Are you cold?" He took the only thing he had, his trench coat, and draped it over her. Then he sat on the edge of the coffee table and leaned over, brushing the hair from her face.

"Do you know why I'm giving the Wild Goose Chase to you, Max?"

"I have no idea."

"Because you know what it's worth. In here." She reached out and put her palm on his chest, above his heart. "You know the emotions that went into creating it and what it represents, even if you do want it to help further your career." Her hand slipped away from him as another shiver wracked her body and her teeth chattered together.

"Great. You've got the chills."

He looked around. There had to be something there to keep her warm.

Of course.

"I'll be right back."

He ran out of the office and returned a moment later to wrap a large warm quilt around her. She took a deep breath, then her eyes opened wide.

"What are you doing? Is this —" She pushed up on one elbow and looked down. "You can't use the Wild Goose Chase this way."

"It's a quilt. That's what it's for."

"But —"

"No buts. It's been wrapped around cold and sick people for more years than you and I have been alive. This is the purpose it was created for, not for sitting behind glass in a museum."

Her eyes returned to normal size and her face relaxed as she eased back down. "You're right. Thank you."

"You're welcome. Now rest. I'm going to shut everything down here, and then I'll take you home."

Izzy smiled, closed her eyes, and a moment later was asleep. For just a moment, Max looked at her, wrapped in the quilt he'd obsessed over for the last few months. Funny how God had used the object of his desire to bring a true treasure into his life.

A dog was licking her face.

Still bleary-eyed from sleep, Izzy pushed Bogie away and sat up. Why was she on the living room sofa? Why was she covered in the Wild Goose Chase quilt? And why was

Bogie standing on it?

"Bogie, no. Get down." She picked him up and set him on the ground. He shook himself and scampered away.

What exactly had happened last night? She remembered feeling worse and worse as she drove to the museum with the quilt. And being in Max's office. Bits and pieces of their conversation floated back to her, and she groaned. She'd made a fool of herself.

"Look who's awake." Using one hand, Janice steered her wheelchair clumsily around the corner from the hall. "You look much better than last night. How are you feeling?"

"Not great, but a lot better. Oh, no." Izzy squinted down at her watch. "I'm late for school."

"Just settle down." Janice motioned for her to stay put. "You were so out of it when Max brought you home last night, I decided to call you in sick this morning. They've got a sub taking over your classes."

Izzy rubbed her eyes, still processing her mother's words. "Max brought me home?"

"He drove your car over from the museum. I'm not surprised you don't remember. You were half asleep when he got you here."

And for some reason, he put her on the couch rather than in her own bed. Probably because he hadn't wanted to venture into her "office" again. "How did he get back?"

"I called your brother and had him come to take Max back." She wrinkled her nose. "That did not go well."

"Let me guess. Brandon refused to let him take the quilt with him."

"Actually, Max never tried to take the quilt. But Brandon gave him an earful. He was still going at it when they walked out to the car."

Izzy looked at the triangles chasing one another across her lap, down to the floor, and back up again. When she and Max first met, they both had wanted the quilt. Now, they both wanted the other to have it. She was beginning to wonder if the quilt carried a Hope-diamond-like curse: whoever owns this quilt shall be destined to chase their tails and run in circles for all time.

"Do you want to tell me why you decided to slink off in the middle of the night to hand over your grandmother's quilt?" Janice quirked an eyebrow.

"I didn't slink. I was tired of all the problems we were having over the quilt, so I decided to give it to Max."

"And you couldn't wait until morning to do it?"

Izzy shrugged. Even she had to admit it wasn't the smartest thing she'd ever done. "That may have been fever motivated."

Janice laughed. "It undoubtedly was. But I can't argue with your decision."

"Really? You think I should give Max the quilt?"

"It's yours to do with as you see fit. At the very least, you should loan it to the museum. But if you want to give it to Max, that's your prerogative."

This was a side of her mother she wasn't used to seeing. Izzy was tempted to check and see if her fever had spread. Instead, she smiled. "Thanks, Mom. I appreciate your support."

Janice put her hand on her stomach and shifted in her chair. "I'm starving. Do you think we could take a break in crisis management for some breakfast?"

Izzy laughed. "Sure. Let me just put this away so Bogie doesn't jump all over it." She stood up and began carefully folding the quilt, first in half, then in half again, then . . . she stopped. There was definitely something hard in the middle of the quilt, right under the two red connected triangles.

She put the quilt on the couch and knelt

beside it, examining the pieces. With her nose practically on the fabric, she could now see that the stitching on them was different from the rest of the quilt. Instead of small, neat stitches, they were longer, looser.

"What's wrong?" Janice craned her neck, trying to see what Izzy was doing.

"These two pieces look like they've been basted on." She prodded the area with her fingertips, trying to make out what was underneath. A moment later, she sat back on her heels, heart pounding with excitement.

"You know how they say X marks the spot? In this case, it seems to be a diamond."

24

Izzy had no problem getting Tara to come to her home, but it took the better part of an hour to convince her to collect the Wild Goose Chase without telling Max.

"I already messed up with that press release," the assistant said. "I'm not going to lie to him on top of it."

"You won't be lying," Izzy assured her. "You'll be helping me with a surprise. When the time comes, I'll explain everything. Look, we both know how important it is for the quilt to be included in the exhibit."

Tara sighed and tucked a lock of silky black hair behind her ear. "He's determined to go forward without it, but he refuses to explain why."

Izzy glanced at the floor. She knew why, but that was between her and Max. "Tara, I want this quilt to be part of the exhibit. The history of it needs to be shared. Consider it my Christmas present to Max and the museum."

The mention of Christmas seemed to strike a nerve with Tara. "Of all years, this would be the one when a Christmas present would mean the most to Max."

"What do you mean?"

"He's always had Christmas issues. I don't know if he's told you, but —"

"He has."

"Oh. Well then, you understand why. But this year, he's different. He doesn't go out of his way to avoid talking about it. He didn't ban Christmas music in the lobby. He even gave me money so I could buy decorations for the break room. Something's changed."

Izzy smiled. It seemed that Max was letting go of the past. "Then you have to take the quilt. It's a gift. Pure and simple."

Tara looked down at the white box on the dining table, clearly weighing her options. "OK. I'll take it." As she picked it up, a smile broke out on her face. "Thank you. This is amazing. If there's anything I can ever do for you, just ask."

"Actually, there is one thing."

"Name it."

Izzy was giving the quilt with no strings, but there was still one thing she needed to make her plan work out. "Can you get me two tickets to the museum gala?"

"I'm sure you're wondering why I called this family meeting." Izzy stood at the end of the couch so her mother wouldn't have to crane her neck to see her.

"Can we just move this along?" Brandon shifted positions on the loveseat and looked at his watch. "I have somewhere I need to be."

"Certainly. Mom already knows this, but Brandon, I wanted to tell you that I called Max's assistant yesterday and had her pick up the Wild Goose Chase."

The explosion she expected from Brandon never came. He just kept looking at her, waiting for her to say something interesting.

Izzy leaned toward her brother. "Did you hear what I said?"

"Yes. You gave away the quilt."

"And you're OK with that?"

He shrugged. "Gran gave the quilt to you. What you do with it is your business."

That sentiment sounded awfully familiar. She looked at her mother, raising an eyebrow in question.

Janice put her hand on Bogie, who was now snuggled between the back of the couch and her hip. "I had a little talk with Brandon yesterday while you were taking your nap."

That fact that she would take Izzy's side and bring Brandon around to her way of thinking was astounding. "Did you tell him about the other thing?"

"What other thing?" Brandon asked.

"No, dear," Janice said with a shake of her head. "That's your news to tell."

Izzy moved to the loveseat and sat next to Brandon. This was going to be fun. "Remember how you thought Gran's note meant that the quilt was a map to a treasure?"

"How could I forget? Not my finest hour." His eyes narrowed. "You didn't find something, did you?"

"A treasure? No. But the quilt did hold the key to something." She pulled a chain from the pocket of her cardigan and held it up in front of him. A dark gold key dangled from it like a pendant. "I found this in the middle of the Wild Goose Chase."

Brandon touched the key with his fingertips. "Do you know what it opens?"

"I didn't at first."

"I said it looked like a safe-deposit box key," Janice interjected.

Izzy nodded. "And that got me thinking that I never closed out Gran's bank account, and that she could have had a box I didn't know about. So I called and talked to the manager. Thankfully, Gran had me down as the beneficiary so he was able to confirm that she did indeed have a box, paid for through the end of next year."

"And that's the key?"

"Yes."

Brandon's eyes practically snapped at the idea that once again Izzy would inherit something from their grandmother and he would get nothing. She recognized the jealousy, but she also saw him fight it down, forcing himself to stay calm.

"That's great. When are you going to open it?"

She put her hand on his knee. "I thought *we* could go open it tomorrow."

"We?" His voice cracked, breaking the one-syllable word in half.

"Yes. You, Mom, and me. Whatever's in that box belongs to the family. We should check it out together."

Brandon smiled, squeezed Izzy's hand, and then looked away. "What do you say, Mom? Are you feeling up to it?"

"Heavens, yes." Janice let her head fall back against the arm of the couch. "I'm so sick of being cooped up inside that I could scream." She looked at Izzy. "No offense."

"None taken. Then it's settled. Brandon,

271

if you can pick up Mom, we can meet at the bank during my lunch break."

Brandon agreed quickly. But then if she'd asked him to give their mother a piggyback ride to the bank, he would have done that too. He was so glad to be included, so excited to see what might be in that box, that she probably could have gotten him to do whatever she asked.

Izzy doubted they would find anything of monetary value at the bank. But there was a reason Gran had hidden a key in the quilt. Something was in that box, something that had been important to her. Whatever it was, Izzy hoped it would finally bring her family some peace.

What Max wouldn't give for a little peace. As he drove down the street to Vibrant Vistas, it didn't look like peace would be coming anytime in the near future.

The gala was two days away, and his life was falling apart at the proverbial seams. His decision to relinquish any claim on the Wild Goose Chase quilt was the right thing to do. He had no doubt about that. But it made an already challenging exhibit even more difficult. It didn't help that Tara had disappeared the day before and now she was acting guarded and distracted. It was like

272

having his right arm tied behind his back. Maybe she was having relationship issues or a family crisis. Max was more than familiar with how distracting those could be.

Steering the car into the retirement home parking lot, Max let out a sigh. The nurse that called him said Virgil was highly agitated. That wasn't an unusual state for many of the residents of Vibrant Vistas, but Virgil was normally calm and even-keeled. He didn't like it when they changed tapioca night or when someone hogged the television in the common room and made him miss reruns of *Matlock.* But the fact that he was agitated enough to warrant a call to Max was troubling.

He strode in through the front door, taking the time to check in with the receptionist at the welcome desk. Then he went straight back to Virgil's room. He found his grandfather pacing the floor, shaking his head.

"Gramps, is everything OK?"

Virgil turned around so fast that he almost ran into the foot of his bed. "Max! I need help."

"With what?"

"I need a tuxedo."

Max tossed his coat over a chair as he moved into the room. "What do you need a tuxedo for?"

Virgil's eyes lit up. "I have a date."

"A date?" Maybe this was more serious than Max thought. His grandfather was delusional. "Who with?"

"Izzy." His thin lips lifted in a grin, rearranging the wrinkles on his face. "She stopped by earlier and said she wanted to take me somewhere fancy on Friday."

"Oh."

"You sound disappointed." Virgil frowned, then his eyes lifted and he slapped his thigh. "Confound it, Max, I didn't stop to think how this would make you feel. I know you've taken a fancy to her. If you don't want me to go, I'll cancel."

Max chuckled. "No, Gramps, that's not the problem."

"Because it's not that kind of a date. She and I are just friends."

"I know. Believe me, that's not what's wrong."

"OK, then what is wrong?"

"I haven't heard from her in a few days, so I'm a little jealous, I guess." Max sighed. "And Friday night is the gala at the museum. I was going to ask Izzy to go with me."

Virgil's eyes narrowed. "You haven't asked her yet and your party is in two days? You can't ask a lady to a fancy shindig at the last minute."

"No, I suppose I can't. It's a nonissue now, anyway." Max squeezed the back of his neck. "What's the big event she's taking you to?"

"I don't know. She said it's a surprise, but it's formal." Virgil moved to the closet and pointed inside. "If it's formal, I need a tuxedo."

Max shook his head. "No you don't, Gramps. Unless you're going to opening night at the opera, a suit is just fine."

"But what if that's where she's taking me?"

"She's not taking you to the opera. Trust me."

Virgil considered it for a moment, then nodded in agreement. "I trust you, Son. The suit it is."

Joining Virgil at the closet to make sure his one dress suit and one tie were both clean, Max pushed down the sour churning in his stomach. Had Izzy purposely made other plans for the night of the gala? And had she included his grandfather to make sure Max knew she was avoiding him? Somehow, she must have gotten the wrong idea when he took her home and left the quilt with her, because he hadn't heard from

275

her since. He wanted her to understand that the quilt wasn't as important to him as she was. But now, it seemed he'd surrendered the quilt and lost the girl.

Virgil's hand landed on Max's back, giving it a firm pat. "Don't you worry, Max. I'll talk you up when I'm out with Izzy." He leaned forward and said in a stage whisper, "Between you and me, I think she's already interested in you."

Max certainly hoped so.

25

Janice and Brandon were waiting in front of the bank when Izzy got there.

"You should have waited inside," Izzy said, hurrying up to them. "It's so windy today."

Brandon hunched his shoulders in his wool coat. "I wanted to, but she refused."

"It's too beautiful out here." Janice looked up at the gray, cloud-filled sky. "I'm enjoying the fresh air."

Izzy looked down at her watch. "As much as I'd love to stay outside and enjoy it with you, I've got to be back to work in half an hour."

Janice nodded. "Then let's go in."

Izzy held the door open while Brandon pushed their mom's chair inside. It took fifteen minutes to contact the right person, fill out forms, show Gran's death certificate, and accept condolences. Then they were ushered into a private area where they waited until the teller brought in a long metal box.

"Here you go," the young man said. "Take all the time you need."

Izzy looked from the box to the key to her mother and brother. She took a deep breath. "Are we all ready?"

They nodded.

"OK. Here we go."

She inserted the key in the lock, turned it, and then slowly lifted the lid.

"Wow."

The box was full. On top was a piece of cream-colored stationery, folded in half.

"A letter from Gran," Izzy whispered. She took it out, unfolded it, and read.

Hello, dear ones.

I have no idea who found the key or realized what it opened, but I never doubted that one of you would. It is my fondest wish that all three of you are here, together, as you open this box. If you are, then I am truly happy.

Izzy had to pause, and when she did, she saw that Brandon and their mother were just as affected as she was. She cleared her throat and went on.

By now, I hope you've realized that the Wild Goose Chase quilt does indeed point to a treasure — not one that can be counted in dollars, but one that is counted in smiles and tears. So many people spend their lives chas-

ing possessions and status; they forget what really matters: the love of our Lord and the love of family. The women who created the quilt knew that, and that's what I want to pass on to you.

I've left tokens in this box for all of you. I hope they help you understand how much you mean to me, and how much you are loved.

By the time Izzy stopped reading, they were all a mess. Janice was sobbing. Brandon was sniffling, his eyes and nose red. Izzy had to hold the stationery at arm's length to keep the tears from dripping off her chin and splashing on the paper. In her heart, she knew the contents of this box held the last gifts from Gran. There would be no more discoveries, no more surprise deliveries. It was a bittersweet moment of completion.

Izzy put the letter down and began to remove items from the box. She handed her mother a small, square jeweler's box with a tag reading "For Janice." To Brandon she handed a permanently curved, letter-size manila envelope. There were two items left. One was a long wooden box with a ballerina painted on the highly varnished lid. The other was book-shaped and wrapped in tissue paper. Silently, they each opened their tokens.

As Izzy suspected, the item wrapped in tissue paper was the final journal. She turned it over, marveling at what she held in her hands. The oldest of the three, this was the one that had started it all. The diary had no doubt been written by the woman who had first stitched the Wild Goose Chase quilt. She couldn't wait to see Max's face when she gave it to him.

She couldn't wait to see Max. Period.

Janice gasped. She removed a gold ring from the box and held it up. The stones, a pearl flanked on either side by rubies, picked up the florescent light in the room. She unfolded the small piece of paper that was wedged inside the lid.

Proverbs 31:10 reads, "Who can find a virtuous woman? For her price is far above rubies" You are a virtuous woman, Janice. Let God light your path and lead you to happiness. I love you and have always been proud of you. Mom

"Help me put it on, Izzy."

Izzy took the ring and slid it onto the ring finger of her mother's good hand. "A perfect fit."

"No way."

The incredulous words from Brandon pulled Izzy's attention back to him. He had pulled a sheaf of papers from the envelope and was staring at them, mouth slightly open.

"What is it, Brandon? Good news or bad news?"

"Great news." He thumbed through the pages. "Gran had stocks. Lots of them."

"That's great."

"No." Brandon shook his head, his voice bordering on manic. "You don't understand. She was holding onto this for a long time. There's some high-value stuff in here. It's worth a fortune."

Izzy smiled. "Looks like you finally found your treasure."

"Read the letter," Janice said. "She must have put one in there for you."

Brandon put his hand deep in the envelope and found it.

Dear Brandon, Thanks to your grandfather, we made wise investments over the years. I know you'll know what to do with these stocks. All I ask is that you consider not only what the money can do for you but also how you can use it to help others. You have a good heart. Let it guide you, and do what's right.

Brandon put the envelope down and grasped the edge of the table. "How could she have known? How could she have known I'd lose everything and need this so much?"

The answer, Izzy knew, was that she couldn't have known. But God knew. And if there was one thing Gran excelled at, it was listening to God.

Izzy squeezed her brother's shoulder. "She was just following her heart, like she wants you to do. A fortune and a challenge." Izzy grinned at him. "Are you up for it?"

"If you'd asked me that last month, I would have said no. But now . . ."

"Now?"

He ducked his head then looked back at her, the corner of his mouth quirked up. "Now I think I can. I might need to come to you for advice, though."

"That's funny," she said with a laugh. "My financial wizard brother needing investment advice from his little sister."

He shook his head. "Not financial advice. Advice about being a good person. Someone who would make Gran proud."

"Oh, Brandon." Behind them, Janice sighed. "You already are that person."

"She's right. You just need a little fine tuning." Izzy bumped him with her shoulder, bouncing off when he bumped her back.

Janice pointed at the wooden box that remained on the table. "What about you, Izzy? Aren't you going to open your last present?"

Izzy shook her head. "Not now. I think I'm going to save it for Christmas."

One last present from Gran. It would be well worth waiting for. And if everything went according to plan in the next few days, it would be a Christmas they'd all remember for a very long time.

26

"Are you sure I'm dressed appropriately?"

Not for the first time, Virgil adjusted the knot of his tie. With her arm threaded through his crooked elbow, Izzy smiled at him. "You're the most dapper man here. And I'm proud to be on your arm."

"Pffft!" Virgil blew out a puff of air as if to chase away the compliment. "I'm the proud one. You look gorgeous, Izzy."

"Thank you."

Once upon a time, Izzy thought this would be a normal part of her life, going to ballet galas and opening nights, wearing dazzling gowns, her hair piled on her head in a gravity-defying style. But when circumstances forced her to change her dream, she'd found she didn't miss the promise of glamour and parties. Her life was simpler than she'd once thought it would be, but it was just as happy, if not more so.

She fingered Gran's necklace, settled

comfortably just above the neckline of her red silk sheath. It had been a long time since there'd been an occasion that she'd needed to dress up for. Like Virgil, she'd wondered if her attire was appropriate for the evening. Thankfully, she seemed to fit in with the crowd of museum patrons.

They reached the entrance. A doorman looked over their tickets, tipped his head in welcome, and ushered them inside. All around, well-dressed men and women talked, pointed at items of interest, and nibbled on hors d'oeuvres.

"This is quite a turnout," Virgil said.

"It certainly is. Max must be very proud."

A white-coated server glided by with a silver tray held up on one hand. Virgil's eyes locked on him. "Do you think they have crab puffs? It's been years since I've had crab puffs."

Izzy laughed. "I don't know, but we can check." She was about to steer him toward another server when a voice called through the crowd.

"Izzy!"

Tara sidled through a group of people and made it to them. "I'm so glad you both made it."

"Are you kidding? You couldn't keep me away tonight. Tara, have you met Virgil?

He's Max's grandfather."

Izzy made the introductions, then looked around again. "Where is Max?"

"Over in that corner." Tara pointed toward the far end of the large room. "He's talking to some of our more serious patrons."

"Good. I have something for him, but I don't want him to see it yet." She patted her bag, feeling the solid mass of the diary beneath the beaded black satin fabric.

Tara grinned. "Speaking of surprises, let's get the two of you out of here until the big reveal."

"Good idea." Izzy put her hand on Virgil's back. "We're going to go somewhere quiet, just for a little while. Then we'll surprise Max."

With questioning eyes, he looked back and forth between the two women. His gaze rested on Tara. "Will there be crab puffs there?"

She smiled. "There can be."

"Then you've got a deal." He looked back at Izzy. "Lead the way, dear lady."

Tara was acting squirrely. Which was totally out of character for her.

Max had wanted to do a last-minute inspection of the Going West exhibit, but on his way to the hall, Tara grabbed his arm and steered him in the opposite direction, into the crowd and straight to Mr. and Mrs. Van Horn. He'd spent the last twenty minutes listening to them talk about their latest excursion to Egypt, how inspiring it was, and why it would be the perfect subject for Max to consider showcasing. The Van Horns were longtime, generous patrons, so Max heard them out, then found a gentle way to remind them that an exhibit about Egyptian pharaohs probably wasn't the best fit for a pioneer museum.

"Would you please excuse me?" He took a step back from the couple. "I need to get ready to open up the exhibit."

"Of course," Mr. Van Horn said with a lift of his glass. "This is your big night, after all."

As Max turned, he heard Mrs. Van Horn say to her husband, "It would be bigger if there was a pyramid involved."

Getting to Hall A was more challenging than expected. Along the way, Max was stopped by almost every person he passed. They wanted to chat, to share about their own projects and ask about the current state of the museum. After another twenty minutes, he was no closer to the hall than when he'd started.

When his cell phone vibrated in his

pocket, he was actually relieved. He excused himself from the group he was speaking with and answered the call.

"Hello?"

"Max. I need you in the exhibit hall."

Sure, now Tara needed him. Where was she when his ear was being talked off? "I'm on my way."

Figuring that people would leave him alone if he looked busy, he strode away with the phone pressed against his cheek, even after Tara hung up. When he reached the hall, she was standing outside the closed doors.

"Is everything all right?" Max asked.

"Yes, just fine." Tara's tone was bright, but her smile was a little too big, her eyes a little too wide. She was hiding something.

"Then let's go in. I want to take a final look before we open it up to the crowd."

She held up her hand, palm out. "Not so fast. There's something I need to tell you first."

He quirked an eyebrow, waiting for her to elaborate.

"The exhibit isn't exactly how you expected."

His stomach flipped. "In what way?"

"Well, you know that without the quilt, it's just not the same."

"I know," he answered with a frown. Without the quilt the exhibit wasn't the same. Without Izzy, he wasn't the same. "But there's nothing I can do about it now."

Tara nodded. "Well, there was something I could do about it. More to the point, someone else decided to do something about it."

"Who?"

"Let's just say a friend of the museum has an early Christmas present for you." Tara stepped aside and opened one of the doors. "See for yourself."

Max's heart raced as he stepped into the room. There was only one person he wanted to see, only one person who would make a difference to him — and it wasn't the man who held a plate of hors d'oeuvres in one hand and waved at him with the other.

"Gramps? I thought you were going out with Izzy tonight."

"I am out with Izzy," Virgil said around a mouthful of crab puff. "This was the surprise."

A flash of red caught his eye.

"Hi, Max."

For a millisecond, his heart stopped. Izzy was a vision in red, her hair cascading over her shoulders in a golden waterfall. She was so beautiful, he almost couldn't speak.

Almost.

"Izzy, I'm so glad you're here. When I didn't hear from you —"

"You thought I was upset." She smiled and shook her head. "We really have to stop assuming that we know what each other is thinking."

Max nodded, hardly daring to hope that she meant what he thought she meant. "Yes, we do."

Behind him, Tara cleared her throat. "I don't mean to interrupt you two, but it's almost time for us to open up the exhibit. And we still have a few things to . . . clear up."

Max looked at her over his shoulder. "What things?"

Izzy put her hand on his arm. "I have a surprise that's going to make you very happy."

Max covered her hand with his. "It couldn't make me any happier than having you here."

Her cheeks grew a shade warmer and she glanced at Tara. "Let's show him."

Tara moved to a tarp-draped display case in the middle of the room. In the excitement of seeing Izzy, he hadn't noticed it. Tara grabbed the edge of the tarp, and with no fanfare whatsoever, yanked it off.

There was the Wild Goose Chase quilt, the centerpiece of the exhibit, just as he'd wanted. "Izzy, you didn't have to do this."

"I know. I wanted to."

"But that's not why I'm interested in you. Not at all." If there was one thing he had to make sure she understood, it was that his heart was drawn to her because of the woman she was, not because of what he could get from her.

"Max, I know." She put her palm on the glass. "This quilt was made to provide warmth and comfort. It was able to do that for my family. By being part of this exhibit, I hope it inspires other families. This is exactly where it needs to be now."

"As long as you're sure." Max stepped closer to the case. Now that there was no question about why she'd given up the quilt, excitement built in him. "I can't believe it's here. Wait a minute." He leaned in, eyes narrowed. "What happened to the red diamond in the middle?"

The laughter that bubbled from Izzy nearly made him ignore the quilt again.

"We have a lot of catching up to do. Short version, I discovered that those two pieces were basted onto the quilt much more recently. There was a safety deposit key underneath." She opened her purse. "And

291

this was inside the box."

He took the tissue-paper-wrapped item. "The last diary?"

"The last one for us to find. The first in sequence." She tilted her head. "A little late, but you can work it into the exhibit eventually."

"This is amazing." Max pulled the tissue paper away and brushed his fingertips against the aged leather. "Thank you."

"My pleasure. And now, I think it's time you let all your other guests in."

She stepped away, but Max reached out and grabbed her hand, pulling her back to him. "We have so much to talk about."

Izzy nodded, her lips curling up in to a contented smile. "Yes, we do. I'll be around after the exhibit. We can talk then."

Max squeezed her hand. "It's a date."

27

The Going West exhibit was a huge success. Izzy watched as people oohed and aahed over the quilt and the posted sections of the diaries as well as artifacts ranging from the early 1800s through 1925, the year the quilt was completed and arrived in California. She kept trying to work her way over to Max but he was preoccupied with a nonstop crush of people. And since he had acknowledged her in his opening speech as the donor of the Wild Goose Chase, she was fairly popular herself. Many of the people came to her, asking questions about her family heirlooms. As she shared how Gran had created a puzzle out of finding the diaries, excitement grew.

Even Virgil got involved. When she told a couple that Max's grandfather had brought the quilt to her, a gift from her deceased grandmother, they latched onto him. Now, he was standing by the display case, telling his story with great theatrical flair.

As the evening wore on and the crowd began to thin, Izzy once again looked for Max. She spotted him across the room, talking to a tall man wearing a black suit and black Stetson. Their eyes met for a moment, but the man in the hat demanded Max's attention. He had to pull his eyes away from her, but Izzy knew he didn't want to.

Finally, the gala was over. The last few stragglers exited the museum and Tara locked the door behind them. She turned to Max, Izzy, and Virgil, who stood in the empty entry area. "We did it."

"*We* is right." Max looked at each one of them in turn. "Every one of you had a hand in making this gala a big success. Thank you."

"You're welcome," Tara said, "although I may regret it later."

"Why's that?" Izzy asked.

"Did you notice the tall fellow in the Stetson? That was Dalton Reed, and he's trying to woo Max away to his historical society in New Mexico." Tara crossed her arms over her chest. "From what I could tell, he was very impressed with the exhibit."

"Yes," Max said, "he was."

Izzy's breath caught in her chest. "Did he really offer you a job?"

Max put his hands in the pockets of his slacks and rocked back on his heels. "He did. But I turned it down."

Tara's hands fell to her sides. "You turned it down? Why? Don't get me wrong, I'm glad you did. But it's a great opportunity."

"Yes, it is." Max looked at Izzy with a smile that melted her heart. "But there are a lot of great opportunities right here."

Virgil stepped up and patted Max on the back. "You're a wise man. And this was a grand evening. Can't remember when I've had a better time. But I'm afraid I'll turn into a pumpkin if I don't get back to the home."

Izzy turned to Max. She'd promised him they'd talk after the gala, but she couldn't make Virgil wait. "I'm sorry. I need to take him home."

"No you don't. I'll take him." Tara walked up to Virgil and threaded her arm around his. "If you don't mind."

Virgil grinned. "Are you kidding? Two beautiful young women in one night? What's to mind?"

Tara laughed. They said their good-byes, with Max and Izzy promising they'd see Virgil soon. As she led him out a side entrance, he was still talking about what a night it had been. "After talking to that nice couple,

I'm considering a trip to Egypt, before I'm too old to get around."

The door shut. The museum was still. Max and Izzy were completely alone. She'd wanted to talk to him all night, but now, there were no words. They just looked at each other, as if caught in a spell that the sounds of their voices would break.

Max stepped closer, his hand held out. Izzy reached for it, and he pulled her to him. They were so close, close enough that she was sure she heard the beating of his heart. Tilting her head, she looked up into his eyes, and she knew. Before his mouth came down gently on hers, their lips meeting in a blissful hello, she knew. It was there in his eyes, so clear, so plain. There was no disguising it. He felt the same way she did.

He loved her.

On Christmas Day, the peace Izzy always hoped for in her home was turned to chaos. But what a wonderful chaos it was.

Virgil sat on the couch beside Brandon, comparing the sweaters they'd both received. Janice sat beside them in her chair, attempting to take pictures with one hand. Wrapping paper and ribbons were strewn across the floor. By the front door, Bogie yipped and danced, trying to shake off the gift bag he'd stuck his head into.

Izzy sat on the loveseat next to Max, their legs pressed against each other, shoulders brushing. It was a moment in time she wanted to freeze and hold forever in her memory.

Max picked up the varnished wood box from the coffee table and handed it to her. "This is the last one."

Everyone else quieted down and gave her their full attention. This was it, the last present from Gran. She took a deep breath and tipped back the lid.

A laugh burst from her lips. "I don't believe this."

The other three leaned closer to see what was inside. Izzy sunk her fingers into the box and pulled out a handful of fabric scraps, each one cut into a precise triangle.

"Are those what I think they are?" Janice asked.

"Quilt pieces," Max said. "Just like the Wild Goose Chase."

Brandon reached out and took one from Izzy. It was white with black blobs. "This is from my cowboy costume."

Virgil looked at him funny. "You have a cowboy costume?"

"Not anymore. It was for a Halloween party when I was six. Gran made the vest for me."

Janice pointed, waving her finger wildly. "And that piece there. The light blue with the pink and green plaid. That was from Izzy's binky."

Max grinned. "Her binky?"

"Her security blanket. For years, she wouldn't let it out of her sight. Then one day, she walked into the kitchen and put it in the trash can. I think she was four."

"How did Gran get it?" Izzy asked.

"I took it out of the trash and told her what happened. She told me to give it to her, that she might use it to make something for you. I totally forgot about it until now."

Virgil nodded slowly. "Looks like she's trying to tell you something."

As always. Izzy looked deeper under the fabric and found what she knew had to be there. "Here's the note."

She unfolded the familiar cream-colored stationery and read the message out loud.

My dear Izzy,

If everything worked out the way I hoped, this is my last letter to you. I told you that the Wild Goose Chase quilt held the key to a great treasure. My desire is that it led you to the greatest treasure of all. Remember what it says in 1 Corinthians, "Now faith, hope, and love remain — these three things — and the greatest of these is love."

Izzy stopped reading and glanced at the man beside her. Max was the treasure Gran had been pointing her to.

He smiled and patted her knee. "Go on."

The pieces of fabric in this box, and the others I've left for you along the way, represent our family. They come from items that were special to you, your brother, your mother, and me. I encourage you to make your own quilt and keep alive the tradition started over a hundred years ago by that first, brave woman.

Izzy, like her, you are strong and brave. I am so proud of the woman you've grown to be. Grab love; embrace it. And count on the Lord to direct your path. He will never let you down.

With a sigh, Izzy folded the paper. "That's it."

"What do you know," Virgil said. "She wants you to make another quilt."

"Are you going to do it?" Brandon asked.

"I don't know. If I do, I'll need some help. *Quilting for Dummies* would be a good start." Izzy laughed as she looked through the fabric. She turned to Max. "Do you have a handkerchief?"

"You know I do." He pulled one from his pocket and handed it to her. "Getting a little misty?"

"No." She smiled, folded the hanky, and placed it in the box. "If I'm going to make a quilt that represents the people I love, then I need something from you, too."

His arm snaked around her shoulders. He pulled her close and kissed the top of her head. At the same time, a flash went off as Janice snapped their picture. Brandon and Virgil looked at each other, then both drew out an extended "Awwwwww."

When Gran died, Izzy had dreaded the upcoming holidays. She couldn't imagine celebrating without her grandmother, who had meant so much to her. But a lot had happened since then. She'd repaired her relationship with her mother. Her brother was making necessary changes in the way he looked at life and what he considered important. And God had brought her and Max together.

Now, Izzy was thinking this might just be the best Christmas ever — the first in a long line of really great Christmases.

EPILOGUE
ONE YEAR LATER

Izzy sat at the dining table, up to her elbows in fabric scraps. Sewing a quilt of her own had turned out to be more challenging that she had thought. Not only did she have to learn the basics of quilting, but she had to come up with a design on her own. Her students had been only too happy to help with that part, resulting in some unusual concepts. It had taken her the better part of a year to get to the point where she felt ready to begin. But today wasn't the day.

"Hon, we really need to clean off the table. They'll be here any minute."

Max leaned out the kitchen door, a wooden spoon in one hand and an apron tied around his waist. It hadn't taken long for her to learn that her husband was a much better cook than she, so when he offered to take over Christmas dinner, she wasn't about to argue.

After seven months of marriage she still

got a zing through her chest every time he smiled. "I'm putting it away now."

He tossed the spoon on the counter, came behind her, and looked over her shoulder. "How's it coming?"

"Good. I think I've finally settled on the direction the geese will fly in. I'm going to start here, at an outside edge." She pointed to a sketch she'd done on a piece of poster board. "Then have the geese move around and inward, until they stop at this square in the middle."

"You're sending the geese home."

She knew he'd understand. "Exactly."

Max kissed the top of her head. "Why is it a square?"

"Because this is going in the center." She picked up the handkerchief he'd given her a year before. "I think I started falling in love with you the first time you gave me one of these. It makes sense to put it right in the center, don't you think?"

"I think you're a hopeless romantic. And I wouldn't have you any other way." He leaned down farther.

She raised her arm and circled his neck, pressing her cheek to his. It was a perfect moment, like so many other moments they'd shared.

The doorbell rang. Bogie barreled into the

room, toenails clicking, barking up a storm.

"Uh-oh." Izzy let go of Max and stood up. She leaned over the table and scooped up fabric and patterns, dumping them in the plastic storage bin she used for the quilt project.

Max put his hand on her waist and turned her toward him. "Slow down. Nobody will care if the table needs to be cleared." His other hand slid over the subtle bump beneath her blouse. "Especially after we tell them our news."

Izzy grinned. "Such a smart man." She rose up on her toes and pulled his head down to meet her kiss.

The front door opened and voices filled the room.

"I told you we could go right in." Janice said.

"Yeah, and walk in on them making out," Brandon joked.

Virgil laughed. "You'd think they were still on their honeymoon."

Max pulled back but kept his face close to hers and his voice low. "We really need to remember to lock that door."

Izzy laughed and greeted their family, pulling each one into a hug and marveling at the change in their lives.

What a difference a year made. No more

chasing after dreams that wouldn't make them happy even if they did come true. No more being haunted by the past. No more wild goose chases, searching for happiness in the wrong places. Now, the only Wild Goose Chases in her family's life were Gran's quilt, once more making its way across the country, but this time in a traveling exhibit, and the quilt that Izzy intended to make.

A new quilt.

A new family.

A new love.

The greatest treasure of all. Just as Gran had hoped.

DISCUSSION QUESTIONS

1. The quilt Izzy's grandmother left her is a Wild Goose Chase pattern. Are there any quilts or heirlooms that have been passed down in your family?

2. Janice Fontaine, Izzy's mom, struggles with disappointment over lost dreams — both Izzy's and her own. How does that affect the way she interacts with her children?

3. Izzy tells Max that she doesn't believe God gave her rheumatoid arthritis but that he used it. What do you think about that? Have you experienced a negative situation that God used to bring about something good?

4. Grandma Isabella promised the quilt to Max but gave it to Izzy. If you were Gran,

who would you have given the quilt to?

5. According to Gran, objects are only valuable because of the memories or emotions they evoke. Would you agree?

6. Brandon was convinced that the treasure Gran mentioned was a monetary one. Why do you think financial success was so important to him?

7. Many people have strong feelings connected with Christmas. For Izzy, they were good. For Max, they were painful. What feelings does the Christmas season bring up for you?

8. In the end, Max has to make a choice between personal happiness and career advancement. Did he make the right choice in turning down the job offer?

9. Even though Gran wanted her family to realize that true happiness doesn't come from material things, she left them material items in the safe-deposit box. Why do you think she did that?

10. First Corinthians 13:13 says, "Now faith, hope, and love remain — these three

things — and the greatest of these is love."
Share a time in your life that represents
true love.

mL   4-13